Diablo –
Last Chance for
Golden Star

Gabi Adam

Diablo –
Last Chance for
Golden Star

Copyright © 2005 Gabi Adam
The plot and the names of the characters are entirely fictional
Original title: Letzte Chance für Golden Star
Published by Pony, Stabenfeldt A/S
Cover photo: Bob Langrish
Cover layout: Stabenfeldt A/S, Elsebeth Christensen
Translated by Barclay House Publishing
Edited by Bobbie Chase
Printed in Germany 2005

ISBN 82-591-1174-8

*For Libra, the colt whose birth was one of the greatest
experiences of my childhood.*

Chapter 1

After their long ride, thirteen-year-old Ricki Sulai and her schoolmates Lillian Bates, Cathy Sutherland, and Kevin Thomas sat at the edge of the paddock admiring their beloved four-legged friends. They were in total, unspoken, agreement that their horses were among the most beautiful, best-behaved, sweetest, most wonderful animals in all the world.

"Just look at Diablo," observed Cathy, pointing to Ricki's black horse. "He really thinks he can get Chico away from that apple tree."

In fact, Diablo was trying to drive the Bates family's little donkey away from the tree so that he could eat one of the apples that had fallen onto the grass. However Chico, who only came up to Diablo's belly, remained stubborn and stood directly in front of the horse, his legs planted firmly on the ground.

I was here first, he seemed to say, his eyes darting back and forth attentively and his mouth dripping with juice from one of the fallen apples.

Given his superior strength and size, it would have been easy for Diablo to force his little friend out of the way, but he just snorted reproachfully and trotted over to Holliday to rub his head on the Hanoverian's neck.

"Thank goodness Holli's color doesn't run, otherwise I'd have a checkered horse in the stall tonight instead of a white one," laughed Lillian.

"Don't tell me you don't like checkered horses! I'll tell Josh!" grinned Kevin. Lillian gave him a nudge with her elbow.

"Don't you dare say a dumb thing like that!" she admonished him, while picturing her boyfriend with his little black-and-white mare in her mind. "Cherish is the cutest horse I've ever seen!"

"And Josh is the cutest guy you've ever met – apart from me, that is," added Kevin as he cleverly avoided being jabbed in the ribs again by the two-year-older Lillian.

"Idiot!"

"Hey, have you guys noticed that Sharazan and Rashid often trot side by side in step? They don't seem to have forgotten their past as circus horses." Ricki just couldn't help admiring the other two horses. They were so beautiful as they ran across the meadow, their necks arched and their flowing, graceful trots parallel to each other.

With each step, Sharazan's mane bounced up and down and his reddish coat shone like gold in the sun.

Kevin's heart nearly burst with pride and gratitude that he was the owner of such an animal. Even Cathy's eyes were unnaturally shiny as she followed Rashid's every move. Carlotta Mancini, a former circus performer and the owner of the dun horse, had decided to let Cathy care for Rashid. The girl wondered if Carlotta realized that she had granted Cathy her greatest wish – well, maybe her second greatest wish – she still wanted a horse of her own. Of course, she'd love to own Rashid outright, but it meant a great deal to her to be able to care for him and ride him whenever she wanted.

Suddenly, the heads of the horses and the donkey shot up as they heard a car driving toward the paddock.

Ricki and her friends looked at each other in surprise. They knew who it was by the speed at which the car approached.

"I wonder what Carlotta wants at this time of day?" Cathy asked, and got up with the others. "Normally, she comes a little later, doesn't she?"

Lillian nodded. "I'm anxious to hear what's up with her," she said.

"Why?"

"What do you mean by that?"

Lillian smiled knowingly. "Haven't you ever noticed that Carlotta comes early only when she has something on her mind that she can't wait to act upon?"

"What? Who? Carlotta?"

"Silly! You weren't listening. Lily meant that –"

"I'm not stupid!" Kevin made a face but then he grinned. "Maybe I know something you don't know!" he said arrogantly. "Don't forget that we live in Carlotta's house! We learn a lot that way!"

"What, for example?" Ricki wanted to know.

"Well, for example, we know when Mrs. Mancini makes a call to a certain Mrs. Charles Osgood Highland the Third."

"You're nuts! Have you had sunstroke?" said Cathy in disbelief. "What could Carlotta have to say to the richest woman in our county?" After all, the woman owns one of the most important stud farms in the state. I can't imagine that Carlotta knows her personally!" Cathy shook her head doubtfully.

"A couple of weeks ago there was a big article about Highland Farms Estate in the Riding Journal. They introduced Garibaldi, that super stud stallion..." Lillian announced.

But before she could tell them anything else, Carlotta arrived. The four teenagers waited as she somewhat awkwardly got out of her car with the help of the crutches she'd always needed since the terrible riding accident she was involved in back in her circus performing days.

"Hi, kids... everything okay with you?" Beaming, she patted Cathy on the shoulder and leaned on her a bit for support. "How's my Rashid? Is he okay?"

"Hi, Carlotta, things couldn't be better!" The girl smiled brightly at the owner of her foster horse. "And you? Everything okay with you, too?"

"Kid, everything's always fine with me," replied Carlotta in her usual optimistic manner, and turned to Rashid. Secretly Cathy rolled her eyes, because she didn't like to be called "kid," but that was a small price to pay for the privilege of being allowed to ride Rashid.

Ricki, Kevin, and Lillian stifled a chuckle as they followed Carlotta and Cathy, who had started walking toward the paddock.

The instant Rashid recognized his beloved owner he whinnied loudly and trotted over to the fence, expecting a huge carrot or a handful of treats, things Carlotta always carried with her.

As she greeted her gelding exuberantly and stroked his forehead underneath the long strands of his mane, she said lightly: "I expect you're all a little bored, aren't you?"

8

"Bored? Why?" Cathy responded a little bewildered. Ricki and Lillian looked puzzled by the comment as well.

"Well, I'm not bored," answered Ricki.

"I'm not either!" agreed Lillian. Only Kevin grinned and groaned dramatically.

"That's too bad," smiled Carlotta. "I had such a great idea about what we could do this weekend."

"Well I'm bored to death! I can't tell you how bored..." Kevin jumped in.

"I don't get it!" whispered Ricki, staring at her boyfriend as though he'd flipped out.

"You eavesdropped, didn't you?" Carlotta raised her finger accusingly, but her smile gave her away, and the boy joined in her laughter.

"Of course! *Somebody* has to keep up with things that go on around here."

"Have you already given it away?" Carlotta wanted to know. Kevin shook his head.

"No! I wouldn't spoil your fun and mine, seeing the looks on their faces!" he said pointedly.

"I don't understand anything you're talking about!" replied Ricki. She was slowly becoming impatient.

"How *should* we look?" asked Lillian.

"The way you'll soon look!" Kevin grinned and rubbed his hands together in anticipation. He could hardly wait until Carlotta told them her big secret.

"Well, then I won't make you wait any longer," Carlotta said, and winked at Ricki's boyfriend. "I would like to send you all on a trip for a few days," she announced, underscoring her words with a determined nod.

"What do you mean, 'on a trip'?" Lillian asked while Ricki looked questioningly at Carlotta.

"What do you think? With your horses, of course!"

"I don't get it. Do you mean we're going on a day's ride, or something like that?"

Carlotta turned to Cathy. "Not a day's ride! I want to send you and your horses on an extended weekend!"

"Well, maybe I'm crazy, but I still don't get it!" Ricki glanced quickly at Kevin, who was almost bursting.

"Carlotta, don't make it so mysterious!" he begged her.

Rashid's owner decided finally to let the cat out of the bag.

"Well, I guess I'll have to be more clear. My dear old friend, Eleanor Highland, the owner of the stud farm under the same name, has a few empty stalls in her stable at the moment, and a really nice granddaughter named Gwendolyn, who's sixteen. Gwen would like to get to know all of you after all the things I told her about you the last time I visited them." Carlotta paused and noticed that the girls' mouths were hanging open in astonishment.

"Wow! You really are friends with the wealthiest, most famous horsewoman in the state? That's cool! You never told us about it," Cathy said, impressed with this bit of news.

"There's a lot you don't know about me! But is that all that you have to say? I thought you'd be happy about it!" Carlotta tapped the ground impatiently with her crutch and then said lazily: "It looks like you aren't interested. You're not bored, so I guess I'll just have to tell Eleanor that you don't want to come."

"Hey, don't you dare! Oh, man, suuuuperrrr! We're really going to spend a few days at that amazing estate?" gushed Ricki.

The girls finally understood Carlotta's offer.

10

"And with our horses too?" Cathy wanted to be sure.

"Are you sure you didn't misunderstand Mrs. Highland?" asked Lillian.

Totally excited, Ricki, Cathy, and Lillian were talking all at once.

"I'm not senile yet! So, what do you think? Interested?"

"Of course!"

"Naturally!"

"When do we go?"

"This coming Friday, if that's all right with you!"

"We would go anytime." Kevin was grinning ear to ear, and his three friends nodded in agreement.

"But don't we have a little problem?" Ricki asked.

"Oh no! How do we tell our parents?" Lillian understood immediately what Kevin's girlfriend meant, but Carlotta just gestured calmly.

"Do you think that I would really bring you an offer like that without clearing it first with your parents?" she asked, and glowered at the teenagers.

"Does that mean Mom is okay with this?" Ricki looked at Rashid's owner apprehensively. She knew that her mother was always anxious when it had anything to do with horses.

"It looks like I've convinced her, doesn't it?" grinned Carlotta.

Now the friends cheered loudly! Full of excitement, they hugged each other and Carlotta. They could hardly believe they would be visiting the well-known stud farm in two days.

"That is awesome!" said Cathy and she gave Rashid, who was looking at her strangely, a loud kiss on his muzzle. "I never dreamed I would get to go there."

"And just imagine, we'll get to see Garibaldi in the flesh! Wow, I can't believe it!" Lillian's eyes glowed.

"But how are we going to get there?" Ricki thought out loud. "It's almost too far to ride, isn't it?"

Carlotta leaned a little more on her crutches and began slowly limping back to her car. Before she reached the door, she turned back to the four friends.

"Don't worry about that! Eleanor is going to have you picked up with her huge horse trailer so that you arrive safely and your horses won't be tired from the trip. So, my dears, now you can prepare yourselves for the weekend. I'm sure you'll love it."

Long after the sound of Carlotta's Mercedes had faded in the distance, the friends were still leaning against the paddock fence staring after her. They were just beginning to realize what a wonderful gift Carlotta had given them.

Three days with Diablo on the Highland Farms Estate! *It's like a dream come true*, thought Ricki, and she sighed with happiness. Meanwhile her black horse held his beautiful head down and grazed on the lush meadow. *I wish I could be as calm as you are*, the girl thought.

*

"I'm sure I've forgotten half my stuff," complained Ricki early in the morning two days later, and she ran back up to her room for about the tenth time to rummage through her bag.

"Ricki, you're worse than your father when he goes on a business trip," teased her mother, Brigitte.

"He doesn't have any problem because you pack his suitcase for him!"

"I would have packed yours –"

Ricki interrupted her. "Oh no, Mom... otherwise I might have a pantsuit or a pleated skirt in my bag instead of my riding pants and my favorite jeans," she answered smiling.

"You didn't pack those awful jeans, did you? After all, you're visiting with society people! Don't you want to look your best?"

"But, Mom, I'm not going to a debutant ball! It's a riding vacation!"

"Ricki looks stupid in a skirt anyway!" jeered Harry, the girl's little brother.

"Harry, you're impossible!" Brigitte looked at her son in exasperation, but Ricki winked at him gratefully.

"For once you're right," she said, and handed him her PlayStation. "Here, kid, for you. Don't break it!"

Harry's eyes lit up. "Wow, awesome. Thanks!"

"I wonder what's keeping the others? I hope they haven't overslept." Ricki was a bundle of nerves this morning and more excited than she had ever been. It wasn't every day that you got an invitation from Mrs. Charles Osgood Highland the Third, owner of Highland Farms, to spend a weekend at her estate with your friends and their horses.

*

A few hours later, William, Mrs. Highland's animal transport driver and personal chauffeur, left Highland Farms with a huge horse trailer to pick up Ricki, Lillian, Cathy, Kevin, and their horses and deliver them to her estate.

"I'm going over to the horses," said Ricki and ran from the house to the stable, where Jake Alcott stood pensively in front of Diablo's stall.

13

"The stable will be empty with just Chico here," he said with a sideways glance at the little donkey.

Ricki knew how difficult it was for the old stableman to be separated from Diablo, whom he had raised from a colt, even for a few days.

"Well, Jake, at least you can rest up for a while," the teenager said, as she slipped into the black horse's stall. "You won't have so many chores to do and we kids won't be underfoot."

"I don't want to rest up," grumbled the old man a little peevishly.

Ricki laid her arm around Diablo's neck, while the horse checked her all over with his lips looking for treats.

"Don't be such a pig," Ricki scolded him lovingly. She wondered whether she should brush him again, but Diablo's coat was already so shiny it looked as though she'd rubbed him down with grease.

"Hello, is anyone there?" Lillian came into the stable corridor and waved to Ricki when she saw her. "Hi, Ricki. Hey, Jake, what's wrong? Is something bothering you?" she asked and, not waiting for an answer, ran over to greet Doc Holliday and Chico.

"Hello, my white giant, did you sleep well? Chico, sweetie, how are you?"

Holli snorted an answer into her hair, and the little donkey gave a happy hee-haw, while Jake muttered quietly to himself.

"Jake is already suffering from horse withdrawal symptoms," Ricki informed her girlfriend. Lillian nodded sympathetically.

"I can understand that. I would feel the same way," she said agreeably to the old man, who still looked disgruntled.

"Just the idea of being away from Holli for one day... oh, I would hate that!"

"Where are your things?" Ricki wanted to know.

"I left them outside." Lillian looked embarrassed. "I was forced to pack much too much," she confessed with a grin. Before Ricki could answer her, the girls heard a car stop in front of the stable.

"The brakes sound like Carlotta," said Ricki with a meaningful look, and Lillian nodded in confirmation.

"Carlotta's driving style is one in a million!"

"Hey! Everything all set?" Cathy stumbled into the stall with her bag under her arm, followed by Kevin, who was just able to catch her as she slipped.

"Slowly, take it easy," he grinned. "Don't worry, we won't forget you!"

"With you guys, you never know," she laughed back and then just let her bag fall to the ground before she hurried over to Rashid.

"Rashid! We're going on vacation today! Do you know that?" she said. The dun horse just looked at her with huge eyes.

"Vacation sounds like at least three weeks," said Ricki.

"Well, I'm not that fussy. After all, three days are great, too, don't you think?"

"Sure!"

"Hey, Carlotta! Are you here to make sure that your Rashid is properly loaded?" Lillian waved gaily to the owner of the dun horse, who had entered the stall as well.

"Greetings, all of you. Are you all ready? I trust our hostess sent a competent handler to deliver the animals safely." Carlotta pulled a carrot out of her jacket pocket and held it toward her horse.

"Who knows when you'll get something like this again," she grinned and patted his muscular neck.

"Do you think I should brush Sharazan again?" asked Kevin as he examined his roan with critical eyes.

"Of course! After all, he's going to be in the company of thoroughbreds today!" replied Ricki, and then she ran to the tack room to check her riding and grooming equipment once again.

"I'm so excited! Three days... three wonderful days at the famous Highland Farms Estate."

"Ricki, calm down!" smiled Lillian. "Mrs. Highland is just a human being, and the stalls there aren't cleaned out with golden manure forks. We probably won't do anything different there from what we do here."

"What do you mean by that?"

"Well, probably we'll ride, ride, ride –"

"That's for sure! But –"

"Hey, I think William's here!" Cathy interrupted her friends, running to the stable door. Seeing the horse trailer make its way up the drive, she was stunned by its size. "Wow, that's a gigantic trailer! That would be big enough for at least eight horses!"

"Well, kids, here we go!" said Carlotta.
Just then Brigitte Sulai came rushing over to the stable. She had seen the huge horse trailer drive up through the kitchen window.

"Good morning, Carlotta!... Ricki, do you have everything – toothbrush, slippers, soap?"

Her daughter made a face.

"Mom, I won't come back a complete mess! Believe me, I have everything I need and I'm sure that I didn't forget anything!"

"If only I could believe that! A little while ago it sounded completely different."

"A while ago!" repeated Ricki loudly, and then she ran after her three friends who had already gone outside and were waving excitedly at William.

"Is this the right place?" asked the driver jovially, sticking his head out the window of the cab as he stopped the huge trailer in the Sulai's yard.

"It depends on whether you intend to relieve a few adults of four annoying teenagers for a few days," answered Carlotta, and the dark-haired man just laughed.

"No problem," he gestured. "Anyone who doesn't behave will be put in a separate stall for safekeeping on the estate!"

"Hey, I think he's a good guy," Ricki whispered to her friends, and Kevin nodded in agreement.

"First impression: super nice!" Kevin said, a little more loudly than he had intended.

"Looks like I passed the test," replied William as he let down the loading ramp. "Let's load your suitcases first, before we load the horses," he said, and pointing to Lillian's bags, he added: "Is that everything?"

The girl turned red. "Hmmm, no! That's just mine. My mother, like all mothers, made me take just about everything in my closet!"

"That's okay, we have enough room. Bring everything over here." William opened a compartment on the lower side of the trailer and began to stow Lillian's luggage.

Quickly, Kevin and Cathy got their bags and backpacks and Ricki got her huge duffel bag and stowed them alongside Lillian's stuff.

Afterward, the saddles, bits, and grooming bags were

put into the trailer. Although it was still early in the day, the girls were sweating from their exertions.

"I'd give anything for a shower," groaned Cathy, panting like an ancient steam locomotive.

"Just imagine how much you'll sweat during the trip," said William.

"Why? Are you such a bad driver?" asked Kevin.

For a moment William was nonplussed, but then he nodded to the boy in admiration. "That makes the score one to zip in your favor. I guess I shot myself in the foot that time. Actually, I just wanted to say that it gets really hot in the driver's cabin of the trailer when the sun is shining as intensely as it is today. The horses have air conditioning, though!"

"Super, then we'll just ride with them in the back!" said Lillian, but William was against the idea.

"Oh, no! No way! You have to suffer like I do! It's against the law, anyway, to ride in the back," he explained to the teenagers. Then he nodded in the direction of the stable. "Bring over your four-legged friends so we can load them safely."

The four friends didn't wait for him to say it again. They ran back to the stable and led their horses outside.

When Ricki appeared with Diablo, William whistled softly.

"My goodness, he looks just like our Garibaldi! I wasn't expecting that!"

"Excuse me?" asked Ricki, laughing as she patted her black horse proudly on the neck. "Well, honestly, I can't imagine Diablo resembles your super stud stallion that much."

"Hmm, do you doubt the beauty of your horse?"

18

"Oh no, she might doubt Garibaldi. Diablo is untouchable," Lillian explained to the driver.

"Well, you'll be amazed when the two of them are standing side by side! So, we've chatted long enough. Bring the animals over here. It's not getting any cooler and we have a two-hour ride ahead of us!"

William took charge of the animals easily. One after the other, he led them into the trailer and tied them up securely.

Diablo scraped his front hooves on the floor angrily, while Holli whinnied for Chico again and again. Lillian had been surprised that the white horse had allowed himself to be loaded onboard so easily. Usually, he fought against any sort of transport with all his hooves. Rashid and Sharazan, the former circus horses, were both completely calm, since they were accustomed to being transported.

"As far as I'm concerned, we're all set!" shouted William a few minutes later. "Do you all have everything? Nothing forgotten? Handkerchiefs to wave with?"

"Man, you're worse than Mom," Ricki joked, grinning. And then she saluted and mimicked a military voice: "Sir, everything's all set, nothing left behind, we can leave! Sir!"

The kids said good-bye to Brigitte and Carlotta, neither of whom held back with good advice and well wishes, and to Jake, who was standing off to the side by himself and observing the trailer with his eyes squinted almost shut.

"Jake, don't look like that," begged Ricki. "Aren't you a little bit glad for us? Anyway, we'll be back in three days."

"I know, Ricki, but I have a funny feeling, that –"

"Don't say that! It's bad luck!" Lillian cut off the old man's words while she tried to comfort him by patting his shoulder. "Just wait. I'm sure you'll enjoy every single minute without our dumb talk," she said winking at him.

"Without your dumb talk, for sure, but without Diablo..."

"All aboard! Doors closed," announced William, and Ricki was glad to escape the pessimistic old man. She gave his arm an encouraging squeeze, took a deep breath, and then ran toward the trailer. These three days on the estate would surely be unforgettable for the four friends.

Chapter 2

They had been under way for about an hour and a half. Ricki and Kevin, who were seated in the front of the cab, chatted happily with William, while Lillian and Cathy dozed on the back seat.

Suddenly there was a loud bang, and the trailer began to sway from side to side. Ricki clung to Kevin and screamed as the edge of the roadway seemed to come closer and closer.

"What happened?" asked Lillian, scared but still a little sleepy, as she was suddenly knocked about on the seat. The sound of the horses stamping their hooves to maintain their balance was heard behind the cabin divider.

"Darn," said William through clenched teeth, trying desperately to keep the trailer on the road.

Stay calm, he said to himself, while Ricki, scared to death, bit on her lips to keep from screaming again.

"Why doesn't he hit the brakes?" Cathy, who had turned as pale as a ghost, asked tonelessly and threw a glance at Lillian, who shrugged her shoulders.

"Who knows? Maybe –"

"The tire... one of the tires must have blown," groaned

William, but he noticed that the vehicle was slowing down, and he shifted gears downward, one gear after another, until the trailer slowly rolled to a stop at the edge of the road.

For a moment, everyone looked at each other in dazed upset and shock, and then, finally, William managed a weak smile.

"Your short vacation has started with a bang!" he said. "Mrs. Highland would have murdered me if anything had happened to you or your animals."

"Well then, I guess you are a lucky man," answered Kevin with a lopsided grin. His heart was still beating wildly.

Diablo's loud protesting whinny jolted the four friends back to the present.

"Come on, let's look after the horses, and then I'll see what's happened with the tires," said William with authority, climbing out of the driver's seat. The trailer was tilted slightly by the edge of the road.

Still a little shaken by the incident, the four teens followed him and waited tensely until he had opened the door on the side of the vehicle. After a look inside, William announced, "Everything's okay! Nothing happened! Your horses aren't hurt!"

Ricki and her friends hugged each other in relief as William went to investigate the damage to the tires.

"Jake had a funny feeling that something was going to happen," Ricki remembered, but Cathy waved her worries aside.

"Jake always has scary premonitions! Haven't you ever noticed that?" she asked.

"Hmm, that's true! But usually he's right. Up 'til now –"

"Oh, come on, people. Stop it. Let's not talk about it any

more," interrupted Kevin. "We had a flat tire, and when it's fixed, everything will be okay!"

"Well, my friends, I don't think it's that simple." William came back around the trailer and had a serious expression on his face. "One tire has blown, just as I supposed, but with all that weaving I must have driven onto something."

"And what does that mean?" asked Lillian, interested. She was looking forward to taking driver's ed next year, when she turned sixteen.

"That means, young lady, that the trailer can't be used. I only have one spare tire, but the trailer has two flats!"

"Fabulous! What now?"

"Now we'll have to think of something," said William with such a funny look on his face that the teenagers had to laugh in spite of the situation they were in.

"You guys can laugh, but I have to think of a way to get you and your horses home safely." Reaching into the glove compartment, William took out his cell phone. "I'll call the garage to see if they have a tire available for us. Otherwise, they'll have to tow us with all the horses inside... that can take a while," he sighed.

Everyone was quiet. But as soon as William turned on his cell phone, Lillian's eyes brightened.

"Wait! I have an idea," she said. "How far is it to the estate from here?" she asked.

"Well, I think we still have about a half hour's drive in front of us," answered William. "Why?"

"Well, I was just thinking, maybe we could ride the rest of the way. After all, we have our saddles here –"

"That is out of the question!" William shook his head firmly. "If anything happened to any of you along the way, I'd never forgive myself –"

"And you'd be killed by Mrs. Highland," Kevin finished the driver's sentence.

"Exactly!"

"Oh, William, we go riding for hours every day. What could happen to us?" said Ricki in support of her friend's suggestion.

The idea that Diablo and the other horses would have to wait for hours until the servicemen from the garage came to tow them was unbearable. On the other hand, Lillian's suggestion that they ride to the Highland estate made her delighted. She loved to ride in places she hadn't seen before.

William was still skeptical, but he had to admit that it seemed to be the best solution for everyone.

"All right. But I'm going to call the estate and have them send someone out to meet you halfway." But just as William was about to place the call, Ricki intervened.

"That's really not necessary," she hurried to say. "If you describe the way to us, nothing can go wrong."

Lillian, Cathy, and Kevin nodded enthusiastically. "Right, and a ride like this is just what we need!"

Four pairs of eyes stared at the face of the driver, who finally gave in.

"Okay. Then saddle up, for heaven's sakes, but if Mrs. Highland tears me apart for this, you'll have to put me back together!" he said.

"Absolutely!" grinned Ricki and started to open the cubby along the side of the trailer in order to get out the saddles while her friends searched in their backpacks for their riding pants and boots. They wanted to ride to the estate in style.

When Ricki finally opened her bag she turned pale.

24

"Has anyone seen my riding boots by any chance?" she asked, moving all of the bags back and forth again and again.

"Nope, I haven't. Where did you pack them?" asked Kevin.

"In my gym bag. The green one."

"Oh, Ricki, you didn't have a green gym bag with you!" remembered Lillian, who had helped William load their things before they left.

"No way! It has to be here! I'm sure, that... oh, crud!" The realization hit Ricki like a slap in the face. "I am so stupid! The bag is in my room behind the door! Darn! How could I be so dumb?!" Depressed, the teenager leaned against the trailer. "To go on a riding vacation in sneakers, that's a first for anyone!"

William laughed, but Ricki didn't find the situation funny.

"Really funny, isn't it? Ha ha!" she scoffed, furious with herself.

"No panicking! At the moment, that's the least of our worries! At our place there are riding boots in every size and variation lying around. We always have guests who want to ride. I'm sure there will be something that will fit you," said William.

Ricki looked at him doubtfully. "Really?"

"Cross my heart!" he smiled, making an X on his chest with his finger.

Although Ricki could breathe a sigh of relief, it was still pretty embarrassing to leave one of the most important riding accessories at home.

"As Mom would say, 'Typical!'" she admitted dejectedly, and then grabbed her riding pants to change.

Later, the friends led their horses down the ramp, saddled and ready.

"We're ready!" yelled Kevin. "Now all we have to know is how to get there!" He looked at William for the answer, and the driver turned to him immediately.

"You can't miss it," explained William. "Stay parallel to this road until you come to the next town, about three miles ahead. Turn right past the church, and then ride straight ahead for about four miles, until you come to an intersection. There will be signs to Highland Farms. Don't try to ride through the meadows. Stick to the roads, and ride beside them."

Cathy nodded. She remembered the conversation she'd had with Carlotta that morning. "Carlotta said that the estate is easy to find. I'm sure that we'll get there with no problems," she said self-confidently as she tightened Rashid's girth and swung herself into the saddle.

"No fear, boss, nothing will happen to us!" added Lillian, patting her horse's neck. "I think we should get going. With luck, we'll be there before noon."

As Ricki and Kevin happily mounted their horses, William watched the teens with mixed feelings.

I just hope everything goes well, he thought. He glanced at his watch. It was 8:45 AM.

"I hope you don't have to wait too long," Ricki called to him, and then the four friends let their horses trot off at a comfortable pace in the strip of grass alongside the road.

William watched them ride out of sight, and then he dialed the number for the garage on his cell phone. After several rings he heard a voice.

"Hello. You have reached the answering service of Smith's Garage. We are closed right now. Normally our garage is open Monday to Friday from eight until noon and from two until six o'clock. We are closed for vacation, but we will return on Monday. We wish you – "

William turned off the cell phone and smacked himself on the forehead.

"Great! Oh well, I'll just have to think of another way," and with these words he dialed the estate. He kicked one of the flat tires nervously, but that had no effect on the time it took for someone to pick up the phone at the Highland home.

*

"When do you think they'll get here?" Gwendolyn asked her grandmother, as the phone rang for the third time.

"I think they will be here within the hour," Eleanor Highland answered as she poured herself another cup of coffee and ignored the ringing.

"Granny, maybe I should answer the phone," offered Gwendolyn, but Mrs. Highland shook her head firmly.

"No! Everyone knows I don't answer the phone before ten o'clock. Anyway, it's probably a telemarketer wanting to talk me into something. They should at least respect my hours, those tormentors! I want to enjoy my breakfast alone with you in the morning, and I'm not going to let anyone ruin that for us!"

Gwendolyn sighed. Her grandmother always stuck to her principles, regardless of the consequences. William knew this and was wringing his hands and praying that she would make an exception today and answer the phone

27

now, shortly before nine o'clock, contrary to her routine. But he waited in vain.

*

"This is beautiful countryside," said Lillian, letting her gaze sweep back and forth dreamily. "It's hard to believe it looks so different here, just two hours away by car from where we live."

"Yeah," Cathy agreed with her. "It's really flat here, and the woods are different than ours."

"It's called flatlands and mixed woods." Ricki held up her index finger.

"Thank you, teacher! But it's true. All around Echo Lake there are only evergreens and fir trees."

"God is accepting complaints!" Kevin took Sharazan's reins in one hand and stretched as wide as possible before he picked them up again. "I'm really tired," he said. Ricki nodded in agreement.

"Well, I woke up pretty fast back there when the trailer began to weave. I honestly thought we were going to land in a ditch."

"Why get upset? William told us in advance that we'd be sweating during the drive."

"Stop making stupid jokes! That could have ended badly!" Ricki scolded her boyfriend and looked at him with reproof, but today, nothing seemed to upset Kevin.

"Could have, but it didn't, and that's what's important. I am so excited about the stud farm. I wonder if they have any foals right now?"

"Oh, that would be great!" Cathy's eyes began to shine. "I haven't seen a foal up close for a long time! Have any of

28

you ever seen a foal being born?" she asked, looking at her friends with interest.

"No, unfortunately, but maybe we'll be lucky this time. I've heard that most mares have their foals at night, alone." Lillian laughed. "I guess they don't want an audience."

"I'd feel exactly the same. But it would be super if we got to witness a birth! Say, do we turn left or right up ahead?" asked Ricki.

"Don't you have any other alternatives?" joked Kevin.

"Nope! What did William say? There will be signs? Well, there's a sign at the intersection that says: Highland Farms Estate, six miles. But there's no arrow pointing the way. I'm getting the feeling that today just isn't our day." The teenager made Diablo stop and she looked all around, confused.

"We should just ride straight ahead," volunteered Cathy, but Ricki zapped that suggestion.

"Sure, but there isn't a road there, unless our noses are crooked!"

"Hmm, we could do rock, paper, scissors... or vote on a direction," proposed Kevin. He couldn't think of anything better at the moment.

"What if each one of us wants to ride in a different direction? That wouldn't help us at all!"

"Well, my instinct tells me we should go right." Lillian sat up in the saddle and stared at her friends.

"Since when have you got good instincts?" Cathy joked. "Oh well, I just hope you're right. Let's go. We can't do any worse than go in the wrong direction. If we haven't arrived by tonight, the estate will probably send out a search party. Nothing can go wrong!" she sighed, and the four friends took up their reins again.

"Didn't Carlotta tell you anything more about this stretch?" asked Ricki, but Cathy just shook her head.

"Well, honestly, I was so excited that I wasn't really paying attention," she admitted. After a while she added, "As far as I can remember, Carlotta didn't mention any roads like the one William was on today. I'm sorry I can't be more helpful."

"Yeah, okay, but you did say at the beginning that the place was easy to find," Lillian interjected.

Nevertheless, she wasn't angry. She looked at her friends with a twinkle in her eye. The day was just too beautiful to be angry about anything.

*

At Highland Farms, Gwendolyn paced back and forth nervously in the dining room. She kept staring out the window at the estate's driveway.

"Child, what's the matter with you today? You're acting as though you had ants in your pants. You're making me crazy with all that pacing back and forth!" Eleanor Highland observed, and smiled at her granddaughter patiently.

"They should have been here by now. They shouldn't have been on the road this long!"

"Now don't upset yourself." Mrs. Highland pushed back her plate and got up from the table. "If you're bored, go over to the mares' stable and look after Sunshine. It won't be much longer before her foal is born."

Gwendolyn's face brightened up immediately. Usually, the first thing she did every morning was to check on her pregnant mare, but this morning she had been so anxious about the arrival of her new friends that she'd forgotten to go.

"Sunshine! Of course! What an idiot I am this morning. I'll go right over to her this minute!"

Gwendolyn gave her grandmother a quick peck on the cheek as she raced by her and rushed out of the house, slamming the door behind her. Outside she came to a halt when she heard her grandmother call to her from the window.

"Please tell Chester to bring Sunshine to the south meadow with Aida and Isis," she called loudly. "It's pleasantly cool there under the trees and also very quiet. Just the thing for expectant mothers!"

Gwendolyn grinned and waved to show that she had understood what her grandmother wanted. She hurried in the direction of the mares' stable.

A little out of breath, she entered the light, generous-sized building where the brood mares were kept.

"Hey, Chester!" called the girl happily to the groom. "Greetings from Granny. She wants you to bring Sunshine, Ai –"

"Aida and Isis to the south pasture," the blond man finished the sentence and leaned on his pitchfork with a meaningful look.

Gwendolyn looked at him, her hands on her waist, amazed once again that he knew in advance what her grandmother wanted him to do.

"Chester, you really are amazing," she laughed. "You must be psychic."

"Well, if you are, you are! But you're too late, Gwen. Your favorite is already outside. We brought her out to the pasture very early this morning. And by the way, I think

31

we'll be keeping her in the stable from tomorrow on. The foal –"

Gwendolyn let out a cheer. If Chester kept a pregnant mare inside, that meant that she would have her foal within the next few days for sure.

"Oh, Chester, that's wonderful!" Enthusiastically she gave the groom a big hug. "Do you think that this time I'll manage to be there when it comes?"

Chester grinned. "Well, if you're not too busy with your visitors it might work out."

"What's the matter with me today? First I forget Sunshine, and now my visitors," she said and stepped back. "I have to go see if they've finally arrived!" and eagerly she hurried out of the stable.

But there was still no sign of the horse trailer. And it was now a quarter past ten.

The girl was becoming more and more nervous and was just about to call Carlotta when she heard the sound of a motor in the distance. She turned around quickly and her face showed her relief as she watched the horse trailer turning into the driveway.

"Finally!" she sighed with relief and waved gaily in the direction of the vehicle.

But her excitement was short-lived. *Why is William going so slowly?* she wondered and wrinkled her forehead. *Something's wrong*. In suspense, she stood still and watched the trailer approach.

*

"That just *can't* be right!" Lillian stopped Holli and looked around in dismay. "I have the feeling that we're going

32

deeper and deeper into the bushes. This isn't really a road anymore, it's more like a path."

"What was that again about your intuition?" asked Kevin, gently mocking Lillian. "But seriously, I'm getting more doubtful by the minute that we're going to find the stud farm in this direction," he added, seconding the girl's reservations.

"If only a car would drive by so that we could ask someone," said Ricki. "But apparently this place is deserted." She glanced over at Cathy, who held up both hands in her defense.

"Well, it's not my fault! There's nothing I can do about it!"

"Nobody said you could! What are we going to do now? Should we go on or turn back and –"

"What? Go back the whole distance? In this heat? Oh no, Lillian, absolutely not! We're at least an hour from the intersection!"

Ricki let herself collapse over the sweaty neck of her horse. The idea that they had ridden almost two hours in this unbearable heat for nothing almost made her want to give up, although normally she could have ridden Diablo for days on end. However, today the sun and the heat had given her a bad headache, and Ricki longed for a cool room, or at least a little shade.

"What do you guys think?" Lillian looked expectantly at Kevin and Cathy, who, in turn, were looking at each other uncertainly.

"I'd keep on riding," replied Cathy after a while. "We have to meet up with someone somewhere who can tell us where we are."

"Somewhere! But you're right," agreed Kevin. "Riding

back isn't going to help us much. Maybe we can call the estate from somewhere."

Lillian grinned. "Yeah, there are a lot of phone booths along this highway," she said sarcastically.

"Look, you guys, can't we just keep going? I have the feeling that my brain is about to fry." Ricki rocked back and forth in her saddle.

"What brain? Don't tell us you have one!"

"Wow!"

"Great!"

"Just stop it!" Ricki picked up Diablo's reins again and urged him on.

"All right, at least the road up there goes through the woods," said Kevin and urged Sharazan to follow Ricki's black horse.

"If only we had something to drink." Cathy swallowed with a dry mouth. "I'm as parched as the Sahara."

"The horses must be pretty thirsty, too. Darn, I didn't think it would get this hot today. Does anyone know what time it is?" Lillian asked her friends, but Cathy and Kevin just shrugged their shoulders.

"We are timeless individuals," grinned the boy, and Cathy held up her left arm as an answer, laughing. All she was wearing was a bracelet. Ricki, however, didn't even react, and Lillian wondered if maybe she was mad.

"Hey, Ricki, what's up?" she called to her, but the girl remained silent.

"She already said that her brain is burned out! That makes it impossible to think, let alone tell someone what time it is," joked Kevin and turned around toward Lillian. "What's up?" he asked when he saw that she had nudged Holli to go faster, on past Sharazan until he was up to

34

Diablo. She had noticed that her friend was slouched down in her saddle.

"Ricki? Are you okay?" she asked and stretched out her hand toward her friend in order to touch her arm. "Hey, what's wrong? Are you sick?"

Ricki shook her head slowly and turned toward Lillian. Lillian was shocked.

"Oh, gosh, you're really white –"

"All of a sudden, I don't feel so well," whispered Ricki with an ashen face. She put a strand of hair behind her ear with a shaking hand.

Lillian rode up close to her and saw the little beads of sweat on her forehead.

"You've got sunstroke, don't you?" she asked, a little scared. Ricki didn't answer. She was dizzy and the road in front of her began to spin.

Lillian took the reins out of her hand and led Diablo as if he were accompanying her.

"Hold on to the saddle or his mane. I'm taking you to some shade."

"What are you two doing up there? Are you practicing?"

"Don't make jokes!" Lillian interrupted the boy. "I think Ricki's got sunstroke. We have to get her into the shade !"

Kevin immediately turned serious. "Wait, I'm coming!" he called, and urged Sharazan ahead and to the other side of Diablo so that he could keep Ricki from falling out of the saddle.

"Shoot, why did I ever think that we could ride to the estate? This area is totally unfamiliar to us," Lillian blamed herself.

Cathy, who was riding behind her, made her feel better. "We all wanted to ride. Don't forget that!"

Lillian nodded, but she still felt guilty about being the cause of Ricki's condition.

"Can you manage?" she asked, worried, but relieved to see that Ricki was at least able to nod. "We'll be there in a minute. You'll feel better then, I'm sure."

Unconsciously, she urged Holli to go even faster, but the horse was suffering from the heat, too. Lillian had to really push him, something she rarely did.

"Is it far from here?" Ricki asked with a faint voice.

"Just a few more yards!"

"I'm so sick to my stomach. I think I'm going to –"

"Hold on, Ricki, we're almost there." Worried, Kevin looked at Ricki. She had begun to weave back and forth dangerously.

Chapter 3

"William! What were you thinking? How could you allow those young people to ride off by themselves? Do you know what will happen to you if anything happens to even one of them?" The voice of Mrs. Charles Osgood Highland III, well-known horsewoman and owner of the prestigious Highland Farms Estate, thundered down upon the driver as though she wanted to crush him.

"But they know their horses and have been riding together for years, and anyway, I described the way to get here precisely."

"That makes absolutely no difference! It was *your* job to bring all four of them and their horses here. It was *your* responsibility, and you alone will have to deal with the consequences if anything happens to any of them or to their horses. Do you understand me, William?"

The driver nodded dejectedly.

"I will throw you out if Gwendolyn's new friends don't arrive safely and soon!"

William stared at the floor. His face had turned bright red from embarrassment and he kept asking himself why he had allowed the kids to talk him into it, when he knew how Mrs. Highland would react. On the other hand, he was beginning to become quite worried himself and wondered why the young people still hadn't arrived at the estate.

"How did you get the trailer repaired?" his employer asked, although she wasn't really interested.

The fact was that William had changed one tire and then remembered that he had a spray to fix flat tires in his repair kit. With this spray he had managed to get the tire stable enough to drive back to the estate slowly. It would have been impossible, however, to transport the horses in the vehicle like this. But none of this would matter to Eleanor Highland.

"And why didn't you call me?" she continued. "At least you could have remembered to do that, or is that asking too much of you?"

"I did –" began William, but Mrs. Highland just waved him aside angrily.

Gwendolyn had been listening to the entire conversation with a funny feeling in her gut. She liked William a lot, and it really upset her to hear her grandmother be so mean to him. "Granny," she began cautiously, but then she saw at a glance that the elegant Mrs. Highland didn't want to be called by that name at the moment. At least not in front of the driver!

"The telephone rang several times this morning. Don't you remember?"

"My short-term memory still functions perfectly!" growled her grandmother, and let herself sink into the nearest armchair. "If only I knew where they have ridden," she said, more to herself than to the others standing near her. "Where is Chester? I want him to take the second trailer and pick them up!"

38

"But, I could –" began William again, but Eleanor Highland silenced him at once.

"You, young man, will do nothing! Gwendolyn, fetch Chester immediately!"

With a sympathetic glance at William, the girl exited the room and slammed the door behind her. She was furious with her grandmother for not even giving the driver the chance to defend himself.

"That's not fair," she mumbled to herself as she ran to the stables. "It's just not fair."

*

Ricki had vomited and now she lay weak on the cool ground in the shade of the trees at the edge of the road. She felt as though her skull was going to burst, there was so much pressure. She felt chilled inside, although she felt the heat of the sun on her skin. At the same time, there was cold sweat on her forehead.

Kevin sat beside her and fanned her with two huge ferns held one on top of the other. Cathy was holding all four reins tightly in her hands, and Lillian was searching the ground.

Suddenly she seemed to have found what she'd been looking for. She ran ahead a few feet, bent down, and then came back with large pieces of dark green moss.

Puzzled, Kevin stared at her.

"What's that for?" he asked Lillian, who had begun to lay the moss on Ricki's forehead and wrists.

"This is damp! Or do you have a better idea of how to cool her off? There doesn't seem to be any water around here," she explained.

"Hey, that's brilliant! How did you know that?" Cathy shouted over to them. Lillian just shrugged her shoulders.

"It just came to me," she replied simply, and then she was silent. While she was watching Ricki breathing with difficulty, she thought back to Jake and his premonition that something bad was going to happen.

"Maybe we should have stayed home," she muttered.

"What did you say?" asked Kevin. But before Lillian could repeat her words, they heard Cathy's excited voice.

"Hey... here comes a car! I'm sure I hear a car coming!"

Lillian jumped up and ran out onto the road. Anxiously she looked back and forth and listened intently in both directions, then she began to wave frantically with two arms.

*

Hey, what's going on up ahead? Mario Mitchell asked himself and squinted his eyes against the sun so that he could see better. He was still a little away from the woods, but he had already seen Lillian, who was standing in the middle of the road, waving to attract attention.

"Something's wrong," the young man said aloud to himself as he slowed down. When he got closer to Lillian, he saw four horses and a boy and a girl standing under the trees next to the road looking toward him. From his car, he couldn't see Ricki lying on the ground, and therefore he assumed that something was wrong with one of the horses.

Slowly Mario drove onto the shoulder and stopped his car. He leaned out of the window with a friendly smile, and Lillian hurried over to him. "What happened?" he asked. "Did you lose a horseshoe, or is it something more serious?"

"Hello! Something worse! Thanks for stopping. You're the first person we've seen in two hours!" Lillian pointed toward the horses.

"Our girlfriend is lying back there on the ground. She's dizzy. I think she's had too much sun."

"What?!" Mario sprang out of his car as though he had been struck by lightning and ran over to the others.

"Hey," Kevin protested, as the man just shoved him aside and knelt beside Ricki.

"It looks like this girl really has had a sunstroke. Can you hear me?" Carefully he stroked Ricki's cheek.

"I'm... I'm... not deaf," Ricki answered in a shaky voice. She tried to smile but she couldn't manage one.

"I'll take you home right away. Don't be afraid," said Mario, turning to Kevin.

"How long have you guys been on the road?"

"I would say about two and a half hours."

"And why are you riding around in this unbearable heat in the first place? Hasn't anyone told you that it isn't good for your horses, or for you? Well, now you can see for yourselves. This is so typical of wannabe cowboys. All riders like you want is to be sitting on a saddle. No matter if it's a hundred degrees or minus ten degrees. And you never think of the animals. People who are as irresponsible as you shouldn't be allowed to ride alone! Who knows what else you might do! You probably don't even know how to ride! Where are you from and where are you going?" Mario stared furiously at Lillian, Cathy, and Kevin, and then he looked at the exhausted horses, wet through with sweat.

"Outrageous!" he hissed, while the teenagers looked at each other, at the same time stunned to be spoken to in that

41

way by a stranger and ashamed that that was how he saw them.

"We're on our way to Highland Farms. Mrs. Highland has invited us, and –" Lillian tried to explain.

"What? Couldn't you think of a better excuse?" Mario wasn't even paying any attention to what they were saying. He was just too astonished by Diablo's appearance. *What a wonderful horse. Exactly like Garibaldi*, he thought.

Finally, Kevin had had enough and he exploded. It wasn't enough that the man had described him and his friends as irresponsible riders, now he was calling them liars!

"What's your problem? My girlfriend is really sick to her stomach, and we thought maybe you could help us! If this darn road were used more, we wouldn't have had to ask for your help. And let me tell you something else, although I don't really have to, the trailer that was supposed to bring us and our four horses to the stud farm had a double flat and we had the choice of either riding or waiting for hours in this heat. There isn't a lot of difference, is there? Unfortunately, we must have taken the wrong road, because the sign back there at the intersection had no arrow pointing us in the right direction! If you don't want to help us, then at least tell us which way to go to the Highland estate! One of us will ride over there and get help!" Kevin's eyes were blazing with anger as he stared straight at Mario.

"Oh, that's who you are? I mean, you guys really are Mrs. Highland's guests!" Mario finally caught on, now looking somewhat repentant. "Oh boy, she's going to kill me when she finds out how I've behaved," he groaned.

"One more corpse at Highland Farms Estate," laughed Kevin, remembering William, who had been afraid of the same thing. "How are you connected to Mrs. Highland

42

anyway?" Kevin wanted to know, and Mario explained that he was one of the stable grooms at the estate, which also explained why he was so concerned about the condition of the horses.

"What luck! Would it be possible for you to bring Ricki there right away? My girlfriend is really pretty sick, you know, and she's not going to get any better as we stand here."

Mario smacked himself on the forehead. "Of course... sure. I... oh, man, I'm sorry I got so worked up a while ago. The girl –" Without wasting any more words, he turned around, bent down, and picked Ricki up in his strong arms and carried her over to the car.

"I'll go with you," shouted Cathy, handing Kevin all of the reins.

"Yeah, but how are we going to get to the estate?" Kevin shouted after Mario.

"Wait here! Don't move! I'll call the estate immediately and tell Mrs. Highland where you are. You'll be picked up within the next half hour. I promise you!"

With these words he got behind the steering wheel, and as he started the car, he dialed the number on his cell phone.

Cathy sat next to Ricki on the back seat and put her arm around her friend. "Don't worry, Ricki, we'll be there in a minute. You'll be feeling better soon."

One last time she waved to Lillian and Kevin through the open car window before Mario took off quickly down the road.

*

Chester was just coming through the door with Gwendolyn as Eleanor Highland picked up the receiver. As the seconds went by in silence, her expression became more serious.

"Thank you," she said. "Chester will leave right away!" Then she hung up and glanced at William darkly.

"One of the girls has had a sunstroke! Mario happened to be driving by where the young people had stopped to rest. He's bringing the girl here. Chester, take the second trailer, drive to Crandall Woods immediately and pick up the rest of my guests. Hurry! William – we'll talk later!"

Chester glanced at Mrs. Highland's driver. He was surprised that she hadn't told William to pick up the guests.

"Get going!"

The groom jumped to attention, touched his cap, and left the room quickly, without saying another word. William left as well. A little while later Gwendolyn heard the motor of the trailer disappearing in the distance.

Eleanor Highland fell back exhausted into her armchair. For a moment, she closed her eyes.

"Granny, weren't you a little harsh with William?" Gwendolyn asked her gently, but her grandmother just waved her away with a flick of her lace handkerchief.

"Let me be for a minute, child. I have to think. Tell me the instant your new friends get here."

Gwendolyn nodded silently and with an uneasy feeling left the room to wait for Mario in front of the house.

*

Ricki lay in bed in a cool, slightly darkened room and slept, after making her friends and her hostess promise not to call her parents. She didn't want them to worry .

44

"It's not that serious," Dr. Burnside told Eleanor Highland calmly. "In two days, she'll be jumping around like a young foal in the meadows, but she should rest today and tomorrow and not overdo it. Her circulation has to stabilize itself."

"What a mess," complained Ricki two hours later, when she was able to think more clearly. "I've really ruined our weekend here, haven't I?"

"Don't be ridiculous," protested Kevin immediately, finishing off the remains of the sandwiches the cook had prepared for them. "That could have happened to any one of us."

"Don't worry about it," agreed Gwendolyn. "We'll just start out the day after tomorrow on our riding tour. I was thinking of going on a two-day trek with you, but we can do that the next time you come to visit."

"What? You wanted to go on a two-day ride with us? So I did mess everything up!" Feeling dejected, Ricki threw herself back onto the pillows. After a few moments she said, "You know, it would be best if William just took me and Diablo back home. Then you wouldn't have to change your plans because of me and you could —"

"Anything else you'd like to say?" Cathy tapped her forehead in amusement.

"I think you're crazy!" Lillian was shaking her head no, too. "Oh no! We came here together and we're going to —"

"You three are going to go riding these two days, and you're going to spend so much time on horseback that you won't be able to sit up straight in the saddle," said Ricki firmly and thought of Diablo. "It's such a shame. I was really looking forward to it."

Gwendolyn looked at each of her new friends. She had

prepared everything for their visit, down to the last detail. The riding trail had been chosen, beautiful shady places to make stops had been found, and the nights in an inn in the country with stalls for the horses had already been booked. The girl had thought of everything and been looking forward to showing her friends the area with all the beautiful spots to see. There was an old ruin of a former Colonial fort, and, of course, the bizarre rocky cliffs that seemed so out of place here in the flat green landscape.

"Well, I guess we should rethink our plans. You just get better, and then we'll talk about it," she said finally, and her tone didn't allow for any contradictions. *I sound just like Granny,* she thought, and had to smile at herself.

"Maybe one day of bed rest will be enough," Kevin suggested, trying to comfort his girlfriend.

"That's for sure," grumbled Ricki softly. She didn't really believe that herself, and that made her mad. Her head throbbed painfully, and she was sure that she wouldn't be able to ride tomorrow, even if she could get out of bed.

What a royal pain! Ricki could have kicked herself, but that wouldn't have done anything to change the situation. Upset, she stared at the pitcher of water Gwendolyn had placed next to her bed.

"You have to drink a lot, the doctor said," ordered Gwen as she put a large glass filled with water into Ricki's hand.

"As if that's going to help," she growled, and then she drank the whole glassful in one gulp.

*

Sunshine paced nervously back and forth along the fence of the paddock. Instinctively she felt that the time for the birth of her foal was approaching. The mare kept turning her head toward her belly and swatting her tail, her flattened croup trembling lightly.

Sunshine was standing close to the fence, and as she leaned against it, a weak spot in the wood gave way and the fence split and broke. Astonished, the mare realized she was free to leave.

Hesitantly, she took a step forward and succeeded in crossing over the remaining lower slat in the fence with her heavy belly. However, she jerked in shock when she touched the live electric fence with her body. With an awkward jump, she managed to get herself beyond the paddock fencing.

Aida and Isis, who were standing a little away from their companion on the meadow, watched Sunshine in bewilderment as she slowly trotted away from the paddock, but soon they lowered their heads to the green grass and went on grazing.

They wouldn't have dreamed of following her. It was too hot to take one extra step.

*

It was one of those beautiful warm summer days when it doesn't get dark until about nine at night. Ricki awoke from a deep sleep about five o'clock. She was feeling much better.

Gwen and the others had saddled the horses and ridden out about thirty minutes before so that Lillian, Cathy, and Kevin could get acquainted with the estate.

Diablo had watched them leave, but couldn't understand why Ricki wasn't going on tour with him, too. Where was

47

she? He whinnied loudly and accusingly toward the open window in his stall, but nobody answered him except Garibaldi, who was in the neighboring stall.

Ricki sat up in bed. She could hear Diablo through the open window. She would have recognized his whinny anywhere.

She got up cautiously and realized with great joy that her dizziness was almost gone. Nevertheless, as she walked slowly over to her duffel bag, which was on the table across the room, her legs were still a little shaky. She wanted to put on a fresh T-shirt and her favorite old jeans. She had to go and see Diablo! No matter what the doctor said. She just needed to be careful that Mrs. Highland didn't see her. The imperious woman would surely send her right back to bed.

While Ricki was getting dressed, she caught sight of a lovely plate of sandwiches and pastries that the cook, Martha, had prepared and left in her room while she was sleeping.

"Oh, that looks delicious!" exclaimed Ricki, and realized at once that she was ravenous. It had been a long time since she'd had breakfast. She devoured the treats with a healthy appetite.

Mmm, that was good, she thought, and she drank another glass of water and leaned back in the chair, satisfied. But she suddenly remembered what she had wanted to do and jumped up. She was just about to leave the room to see Diablo, when she heard a commotion under her window.

"Huh, what's going on?" she murmured and went closer to hear better what had caused the tumult.

Chester was standing below on the gravel driveway gesticulating wildly with his hands.

48

"I was just about to get the pregnant mare from the pad-dock, and only Aida and Isis were there! The fence poles were rotted in some places and it looks like Sunshine got out! Good heavens, that mare is very pregnant and near term! Where is Mario? We have to look for that animal!"

Jim, another of the stable hands, turned pale.

"Are you kidding? The best mare in our stable is miss-ing? Oh shoot! Look out! Mrs. Highland will never forgive you! She's furious with William as it is, because of that girl with the sunstroke!"

"Shut up, will you! It's not my fault! After all, the fence was still intact this morning, and normally – Oh, there's Mario!"

Chester explained to his fellow groom what had hap-pened, and ended by saying, "At least we still have Aida and Isis in the stable. But we've got to get going and find Sunshine right away!"

Mario nodded emphatically.

The three men ran off, and soon after, Ricki saw two Jeeps drive out of the driveway so quickly that they left a cloud of dust behind.

She was shocked by what she'd discovered in that con-versation and she leaned back against the wall feeling a lit-tle unsteady.

Near term, she thought, and closed her eyes for a mo-ment. *Heavens, if she is out somewhere and runs onto the road or... or if maybe she has her foal somewhere where no one finds her... Oh man, where in the world are Kevin and the others? I have to find them so that they can join the search for Sunshine.*

Determined to find her friends, Ricki opened her eyes again and quietly left her room. She kept looking all

49

around, cautiously, so that no one would notice her and send her back to her bed, but the huge house seemed completely empty.

Undiscovered, Ricki ran toward the stables. If only she knew where her friends were and where Diablo had been quartered! But she hadn't been around when he had arrived at the estate.

After looking into three different stables and not finding her horse, Ricki had one last possibility to find Diablo.

"Diablo... Diablo... where are you?" she called loudly across the yard, in spite of the danger of being discovered. In the next instant a joyous whinny answered her.

Ricki smiled and ran toward the sound. Less than three minutes later, she was running down a stable corridor, which was as clean as a whistle, toward her beloved black horse, who had stretched his head far over the top of his stall toward her.

"There you are, my boy," she greeted him with a sigh of relief. She opened the sliding door of his stall and took his head lovingly in her arms. "Wow, someone really gave you a good brushing this morning, didn't they?"

Where have you been all this time? Diablo seemed to ask, and nudged her impatiently with his soft nose.

"You have no idea where the others went?" Ricki asked her horse and looked around. The three stalls nearby were open, and Ricki assumed that Sharazan, Rashid, and Doc Holliday were being ridden.

"Terrific! What are we going to do now?" Pensively she looked at her horse.

"Somewhere out there is a very pregnant Sunshine. What if those men don't find her?" Ricki, who loved horses beyond everything else, couldn't help thinking and worrying about the mare. She chewed on her lower lip nervously and then made a spontaneous decision.

"How do you feel about us joining the search for Sunshine?"

Diablo didn't know who she meant by that name, but he could tell by the sound of her voice, which he knew so well, that she intended to go riding with him, and that pleased him very much. Happy, he neighed, and threw his head back in anticipation, making his long mane fly back and forth.

"I feel the same way," grinned Ricki, although she didn't really feel like laughing.

She always found it astonishing that Diablo seemed to understand exactly what she wanted.

"Now all you have to do is tell me where your saddle is. The tack room must be around here someplace. I'll be right back."

Quickly Ricki shut the stall door and went to look for it. It wasn't long before she found what she had been looking for.

She took her saddle and hurried back to Diablo, who was waiting for her excitedly.

Ricki was glad that she didn't have to groom her horse, and so she put the saddle on Diablo's back.

A few moments later she lead him out into the yard, tightened the girth, and then rode off, still unseen, between the stables and into an area unknown to her.

"Well, let's try our luck, okay, sweetie?" she said, and patted the muscular neck of her horse lovingly.

The doctor's instructions to rest were forgotten, but after only a half hour, Ricki began to notice, to her dismay, that every step Diablo took gave her a sharp pain in her head.

She led her horse to the shoulder along the road to soften the horse's steps. She wished she were back in bed, but the thought of the pregnant mare made her go on.

*

In the meantime, Sunshine had wandered a considerable distance from the paddock. She had headed for the cliff through a small woods and over a wide meadow. It was the same location that Gwendolyn had wanted to show her guests.

It was some distance from the estate, but the mare had finally found a place where she could have her foal in peace without curious onlookers. In the last two days, she had delayed the birth on purpose because there had always been too many people around her – many more than usual.

Of course she liked Mario and Chester, who took good care of her, and she loved Gwen, who always brought her a treat whenever she visited her. But for the birth of her foal she wanted to be alone.

Sunshine felt that her foal was anxious to see the light of this world, and the pressure on her belly grew stronger from one minute to the next.

Nervously the mare paced back and forth, every once in a while letting out a deep groan as she hit her hind hooves against her belly, as though she could get rid of the pain that way.

The beginning labor pains reminded her of the colic she'd had a few weeks earlier when she'd gotten out and eaten too many unripe apples in the orchard on the estate.

Her neck and the inside of her haunches were covered in sweat as she wearily found her way between the huge boulders. Then she stopped abruptly on a small plateau and lay down awkwardly. She stretched her head upward and looked at the bright blue sky. The labor pains, which were coming in ever-shorter intervals, made her whole body tremble.

Chapter 4

Gwendolyn, Kevin, Lillian, and Cathy had galloped happily across a long meadow with their horses. Although he was in good spirits, Kevin missed Ricki a lot. He had told the girls jokes during the entire ride, but his thoughts kept going back to his girlfriend, stuck in bed in her room at the Highland estate.

I should have stayed with her, the boy thought. *It's not fair that she couldn't come riding with us.*

"Hey, Kevin, what's up? Are you dreaming about riding with a bunch of cute girls?" Cathy giggled, as he let out an unconscious deep sigh.

"Of course not! I was just thinking about Ricki!"

"Well, gee, this bunch of cute girls thanks you for the compliment!"

"Really, though, it's a bummer that she can't be with us," Lillian agreed, ignoring Cathy's sarcasm, and bent her head back so that the late rays of sunshine could tickle her face.

"Do you think that she'll be better tomorrow and able to ride with us?" asked Kevin, and Gwen realized that there was more than just a simple friendship between him and Ricki.

"Well, you heard what the doctor said."

"Hah, he doesn't know Ricki," laughed Cathy. "That girl is as tough as nails! I'm positive that she won't let anyone keep her from mounting her beloved Diablo. I'd bet my entire month's allowance on that!"

"Allowance? What's that?" grinned Kevin, who was notorious for always being broke. He spent everything on treats for Sharazan and new CDs.

"Hey, look!" Gwen pointed to the right, where the unusual rocky cliff formations were visible. "Isn't that beautiful?" She had led her guests along a winding path in the direction of the point of interest that impressed everyone who saw it.

"Wow, that's gorgeous!" Lillian said. "Can we ride over there, or is it already too late today?"

"Hmm," Gwen deliberated for a moment, "It will take us about forty-five minutes to ride over there for sure, but if we take the direct path back to the estate afterward, I'm sure we can be back in time for dinner."

"Well, then, what are we waiting for?" enthused Cathy as she urged Rashid forward.

*

"Hudson... HUDSON! Where in the world are you?" Eleanor Highland's booming voice could be heard throughout the house.

The gray-haired butler, who was standing in the kitchen, rolled his eyes. "She's been getting on my nerves today," he grumbled. "She must have forgotten that she asked me to bring that girl, Ricki, a cup of tea in her room."

Martha, the cook, smiled as she poured the tea into a delicate English china teapot and put it on the silver tray beside the matching cup and saucer. "Don't let her bother you!" she replied. "After all, you only have two hands!"

Hudson sighed. "Two hands are not nearly enough if you work for Her Highness. She expects double work from all her employees."

"Don't I know it!"

Obediently Hudson picked up the tray, on which Martha had also placed a plate of just-baked cookies and a lovely bud vase with one perfect pink rose.

"Wish that girl a speedy recovery from me," she shouted after Hudson as he left the kitchen and disappeared from sight.

*

"Good gracious, where were you? Do you want to let our sick guest die of thirst?" Mrs. Highland reprimanded the butler as he came up the winding staircase to the second floor where Ricki's room was located. "I'm getting the feeling that I have to do everything myself around here! I wonder why I bother to hire help in the first place?" fumed Mrs. Highland and reached out for the tray. "Give it to me, and make sure that dinner is ready on time!"

"Might I mention," began Hudson, "that Miss Gwendolyn and the young people are still out riding. Should I... ?"

"Do as I tell you! My granddaughter will be back on time. She knows when we eat!"

Hudson nodded in acquiescence and turned to go. With tray in hand, Mrs. Highland walked the few feet to Ricki's room and pressed down the door handle with her elbow.

56

"Hello, young lady, would you like some –? What on earth! Where is she? HUDSON! HUDSON!"

Less than two minutes later she gave her butler orders to search every room in the house for Ricki.

"And if you don't find her here, then look in the stables! That girl should be in bed! I don't want to even think about what could happen to her. She could collapse again! And send Chester to me. I want to know how Sunshine is!"

"Very well, ma'am" mumbled Hudson, and hurried away, out of the reach of "Her Highness."

"We seem to be in a particularly foul mood today," he murmured to himself. Then he began to open the door of one room after another and look inside, but, right from the start, he had the feeling that he wasn't going to find Ricki.

*

Ricki's headache was becoming more unbearable, and it was making tears come to her eyes. For one moment she was tempted to turn her horse around and ride back to the estate. But then, in her mind's eye, she saw the pregnant mare, and she clenched her teeth and pressed her calves more firmly into Diablo's belly.

"Come on, my boy, we have to find her! Can't you turn on your internal radar?" she asked her black horse and stroked his mane lovingly as he began to trot faster.

Like a jackhammer! thought Ricki and groaned softly. *There's a construction site inside my head! Maybe I'm riding around here for nothing... maybe the men have already found the mare, and she's back in her stall, safe and sound.*

After a while, Ricki reined Diablo to a stop so she could take a good look around – and stop the awful throbbing.

"What do you think?" she asked her four-legged friend. "Sunshine could be anywhere, couldn't she? Do you think it makes any sense to go on looking?"

Diablo threw his head back and whinnied shrilly, and tried to get her to loosen the reins. He danced around in his excitement, and just then he caught an unfamiliar scent. He jerked to a stop and flared his nostrils. His body trembled, and Ricki, who knew her gelding very well, knew by his behavior that he had discovered something that she wouldn't be able to see for some time yet.

"Well, come on, tell me. What's up? Do you have any idea where Sunshine is?" Ricki hoped that was so, but she knew that it would be a coincidence if he did. After all, this area was totally new to them both, and, especially for Diablo, there was sure to be a lot of things to discover.

The black horse whinnied again and trotted off before Ricki could even give him a signal. As a matter of habit, she stopped him immediately.

"Hey, what's the big idea?" she asked a little angrily. "Where do you think you're going?!"

Diablo turned his head toward her and looked at her with his wise eyes. *Don't get mad at me all of a sudden,* he seemed to say, *Trust me... after all, I have a better sense of smell than you do, don't I?*

Ricki sighed and gave him his head. "Sorry," she murmured. "You probably have your reasons. So, where do you want to go?"

After some hesitation, Diablo trotted straight across a meadow, toward the high cliffs beyond.

"Why do you want to go there?" asked Ricki and tried to soften the steps of her horse by posting, but the jolting in her head was starting to make her dizzy.

Why do I have to have such a soft head? Today of all days, she thought, and wished that Kevin and the others were there.

Suddenly she heard the neighing of a horse in distress, and the sound made Diablo break into a gallop. He didn't seem to hear Ricki's groans, but galloped on, faster and faster.

Just don't fall off now, she commanded herself as she held on tightly to Diablo's mane, trying not to let the dizziness overcome her.

Diablo galloped directly toward a narrow path that seemed to meander through the cliffs, and Ricki closed her eyes in fear as she realized that her horse wasn't slowing down, even though the boulders were getting closer.

"Diablo... DIABLO! For heaven's sake, slow down!" screamed Ricki, pulling desperately on the reins, but her horse ignored her order as though she had simply tugged at his mane.

Just as Ricki thought they would smash into the rocky wall, Diablo came to a complete four-legged stop, so abruptly that Ricki practically slid out of the saddle. She avoided falling off only by clinging to her horse's neck, which was straight up as he sniffed the air.

"Are you crazy?" Trembling, the girl slid off of the horse. "I'm really beginning to think I should have listened to Jake and not come here," she said quietly, and looked in bewilderment at her horse, who never before had put her in danger.

After she had caught her breath and stopped shaking, she decided to give in to Diablo's impulse and venture at least partway down the narrow trail.

Excited, the black horse continued to whinny in the

59

same direction, but no answer could be heard. Ricki started down the path on foot, with her horse on the lead.

*

"Wow, this place is really something," exclaimed Cathy, when she and her friends had arrived in front of the cliffs. "I'd love to climb around. There must be a wonderful view from up there."

"I wouldn't do that," said Gwen. "The cliffs are as slippery as ice as you go up higher."

"How do you know that?" Kevin was interested to know.

"Well, do you think I never had the idea to climb up here? Anyway, it's forbidden. Didn't you see the warning signs?"

Lillian grinned. "Nope, we never see those kind of signs, on principle. No one said that we wanted to do any real rock climbing, but I have to admit, I wouldn't mind doing a little bit of climbing, just for fun."

"Oh, come on, Gwen, don't be a wimp. No one will find out that we did a little climbing."

"Not me!" Gwen made a face. "Have you thought about your horses? Did you intend to have them climb up those steep paths as well?"

"Of course not! We're not that stupid." Kevin thought about what Gwen said for a few moments and then snapped his fingers. "I've got it! Since you don't want to go with us anyway, you could take care of our horses, okay?"

Gwen rolled her eyes and sighed in resignation. She realized that her new friends had already decided to climb in spite of her warning and the signs.

"Oh, well... but don't say later that I didn't warn you about the dangers of climbing in those cliffs."

"You said that so elegantly." Cathy laughed, as she jumped down from Rashid's back. Lillian and Kevin dismounted as well, and after a short pause, Gwen got down from the saddle, too, so that she could hold the reins of the other horses.

"We won't stay long," Lillian promised the worried-looking teenager.

"And we'll make sure nothing happens," added Cathy.

"Don't worry," called Kevin over his shoulder. But as Gwen watched the three take off, she could imagine all kinds of things that could happen.

"I have a bad feeling about this," she whispered to her gelding, Black Jack, who was busy sniffing Doc Holliday.

*

Philip Hudson had searched the two floors of the large house for Ricki, but to no avail. So he decided to go to the stables to tell Chester that Mrs. Highland wanted to see him.

The grooms were usually in the tack room at this time of day, cleaning and polishing the harnesses. So Hudson was very surprised that he didn't run into anyone.

"That's impossible," he mumbled softly to himself, and searched the entire corridor through the stable. "Huh? None of the guests' horses are here either. Well, maybe Gwen saddled the black horse so that she could exercise him."

For a moment Hudson just stood there undecided, but then it occurred to him that the groom might be in the mares' stable. *Maybe Sunshine is giving birth right now and Chester is with her,* he thought.

Quickly he left the guests' stalls to run over to the mares' stable, but when he arrived, only Aida and Isis were there to greet him. Sunshine was nowhere to be seen, nor were Chester, Mario, or Jim.

I'm beginning to get the feeling that something is very wrong, thought Hudson, and he decided to inform Mrs. Highland immediately, before her bad temper caught up with him because he hadn't let her know in time about what he had observed.

*

Ricki had trouble keeping up with Diablo as he pushed forward on the narrow trail.

"Now come on, go a little more slowly," she begged him again and again, but the farther the black horse went, the more agitated he became, and his two-legged friend could hardly hold him.

All of a sudden, he stopped short and flared his nostrils. Quietly, he whinnied.

"What's wrong?" asked the girl, and she stroked Diablo's muscular neck to calm him. She leaned on him for a few seconds and pressed her still-throbbing head into his coat, but the horse shied away from her.

Then Ricki caught a glimpse up ahead, where the trail came out of the cliffs and ended in a small plateau.

Diablo neighed again, this time much more loudly, and this time there was a soft but unmistakable answering neigh.

At first Ricki thought it wasn't possible. How could a

horse get onto this plateau among the cliffs? After all, there were hardly any wild horses around... or maybe there were.

In any event, Ricki didn't feel comfortable. She imagined herself between Diablo and a strange horse, and knew it was not a good place to be. Once again she wished she were back in bed on the estate.

"What a day," she whispered, but she was curious, so, she gathered Diablo's reins in her hands and slowly moved ahead.

After a few feet she stopped her horse and stared in disbelief onto the rocky ledge just in front of her. *Sunshine! That must be Sunshine lying there. Oh my God, she's lain down here to give birth to her foal! That's terrible! She's lying too close to the edge. If she falls down... or... if the foal – Oh God, what should I do?*

Ricki's thoughts were running away with her. She was so worried about the animal and the baby horse that was obviously about to be born. Frightened, the girl covered her mouth with the palm of her hand to prevent herself from making any sound that would scare the mare.

Even Diablo seemed to understand the danger and he kept shaking his head excitedly, but he didn't whinny. Cautiously he dug his front hoof into the stony ground to get a secure foothold, and then he stood completely still, like a statue, with his gaze directed on the brown mare, who lay groaning on her side and kept raising her head toward her belly.

From the side, Sunshine noticed Ricki and Diablo, and she would have liked to get up and find another place in which to foal, but she knew that she was no longer able to do that, since the contractions had grown much stronger and closer together. Her foal would be born here.

Ricki, who had never witnessed the birth of a foal, was scared to death, as suddenly the mare's water broke and poured out of her body.

"Oh, good grief, Diablo... is that normal? What... what... oh no... if only the others were here!" Ricki panicked at the sight of the beginning birth, but her love of horses and her desire to help any animal in pain made her swallow her fear. When she let go of Diablo's reins in order to go over to the mare, the black horse blocked her way. He seemed to know instinctively that Ricki shouldn't interfere.

The girl understood what her horse was trying to tell her, and, although upset, she stood frozen where she was. The only thing that could help her and, hopefully, the mare as well, were the prayers Ricki sent heavenward, with a plea that the birth should go well.

"Dear God, "she prayed, "I will do without my allowance for the rest of my life, if everything goes okay."

*

Kevin climbed happily up onto a ledge. "I almost feel like that famous mountain climber with a beard. What was his name?" he joked.

"I have no idea, but he would probably laugh himself silly if he saw us panting here on these rocks!" replied Lillian, breathless but just as happy.

"You are so out of shape," grinned Cathy, who was climbing like a monkey, but the exertion showed on her face as well.

"When we have fifteen more feet behind us, I bet the view will be worth it. I think we should take a break up there for a minute, and then go back down. Gwen will be relieved to see us again," said Kevin, while he continued zigzagging upward.

"Fifteen more feet? So far?" Lillian rolled her eyes.

"Don't complain. That's exactly the same distance you'd travel if you mounted Holli five times, one after another!"

"At least this cliff stands still when I put my foot in the stirrup – I mean on the ledge."

"Made it," cheered Kevin, taking his last step onto the plateau. He let his body sink to the ground and tried to catch his breath. A few seconds later, however, he jumped up again and raised his arms into the air while his eyes scanned the panorama around him. "Wow, this view is really incredible," he exclaimed and whistled loudly.

The two girls, who had arrived at the top as well, turned all the way around and were so astounded by the magnificence of the view that they could hardly believe their eyes.

"Do you two feel this sense of unlimited freedom, too?" the romantic Lillian asked, but instead of a direct answer, Kevin responded somewhat sadly, "I wish Ricki were here... She'd love it."

Cathy, who was just about to say something, hesitated, and then put her hands to her forehead to shield her eyes from the glare of the sun and stared straight ahead. Grinning, she turned back to the others.

"Your wish has been granted, brave Kevin," she sang, and the boy looked at her as though she were crazy.

"Huh? What is your problem? Is the air too thin for you up here?"

Cathy kept grinning and pointed at the opposite ledge.

"Unless I'm wrong, Ricki is standing over there with Diablo... and she's standing over a horse that's lying on the ground!"

"What!? Have you seen a mirage, or just flipped out?"

"Oh, don't be ridiculous! I'm not an idiot... open your eyes!"

Kevin and Lillian looked meaningfully at each other before they looked in the direction Cathy was pointing.

"You're right! That is Ricki! What's she doing here? I thought she was lying obediently in bed and recuperating, but instead, she's hanging out there with Diablo." Kevin shook his head in wonder, unable to believe what he was seeing.

"That horse... Cathy's right... there's a horse lying on the ground in front of her!" Lillian was very excited. "We have to see what's going on there! Come on! I have the feeling that Ricki needs our help."

Cathy nodded. Her face had turned pale and frightened, and Kevin looked worried as well.

The three friends began to climb down as quickly as they could and hoped that Gwen would know the way to the ledge where Ricki was standing with the horses.

*

Gwendolyn looked at her watch nervously. More than half an hour had passed since Cathy, Lillian, and Kevin had begun their climb.

It's about time they were back here, the sixteen-year-old murmured to herself. Her stomach had begun to grumble, and she was getting hungry. Even the horses were getting impatient, stepping from one leg to the other.

"It's okay, sweetie pies. You're hungry, too, aren't you? Don't worry, at home a large armful of hay and some oats are waiting for you –"

A shrill scream interrupted the quiet and, terrified, Gwen choked on her words.

Rashid's head jerked upward and his ears pointed up before he whinnied.

"Stay calm," said Gwen to the very tense dun horse, even though she herself felt a little scared and had to keep her hands from trembling. Hadn't she had a funny feeling at the beginning that something would happen?

Gwen thought about what to do. She could tie up the horses to a tree growing at the foot of the cliffs so that she could look for her friends, but she hated to tie them up with the reins; it was just too dangerous.

With a heavy heart, she could do nothing but wait and hope that the scream hadn't meant anything.

*

Holding her breath in fear and fascination, Ricki stood there and watched the beginning birth with a look of wonder and awe on her face. She saw the strong spasms seize the belly of the mare as the animal tried to push out the foal.

Ricki had the feeling that she was experiencing the mare's pain in her own body. Diablo, on the other hand, had lowered his head and was dozing indifferently.

A portion of the foal's front legs was already visible.

"You'll be okay," whispered Ricki, both to give herself courage and to encourage Sunshine. "You're doing fine! You're a wonderful horse and your foal is the most beautiful foal in the whole world... Come on, keep going... everything's okay!"

But nothing was okay!

67

Ricki and Diablo both jerked as they heard the scream that echoed off the walls of the cliffs, but the girl would never have thought in a million years that it was Cathy's voice.

She was much too busy watching the mare, who had been so alarmed by the loud human voice that she was now trying to get up to flee, in spite of the fact that the birthing had already begun. She kept falling back down onto her side and was beginning to panic.

"Oh no!" Ricki exploded and let go of Diablo's reins.

"Stand still," she pleaded with her horse as she went slowly, one step at a time, toward the mare. All the while she kept talking calmly to the frightened animal and hoping that she would get to her before she managed to get up on her feet.

Chapter 5

"Say that again!" demanded Mrs. Highland III, hoping that she had misunderstood him, as Hudson once again gave her his truthful report.

Overcome at the news, she collapsed into an armchair. She needed a moment to think. But in no time she pulled herself together.

"This is simply unbelievable," she said, exasperated. "My young guest has ridden off with her horse, God only knows where; the grooms are nowhere to be found; and my best pregnant mare has disappeared. Have I gone crazy?"

Hudson, a noncommittal expression on his face, thought it best to remain silent.

"What are you waiting for, for heaven's sakes? Get a car and get going! They have to be somewhere! I can't stand thinking about it. Tell William as well, and don't come back until you've found someone! Understand?"

Hudson nodded and left the sitting room. Sighing, he made his way to William's room in the wing of the house reserved for the live-in help. He hadn't planned to spend his weekend just driving around aimlessly.

"I might as well forget about spending the evening with

Martha, and you'll have to cancel your poker game!" he greeted William, as the younger man opened his door.

*

"It hurts so much," whimpered Cathy, who was sitting on the ground and hugging her left leg, her face twisted in pain.

"How did it happen?" Lillian asked. She knelt beside Cathy and tried to help. Kevin examined the injured ankle carefully.

"No idea, it all happened so fast. The stone I stepped on was loose. I think it rolled out of place. Ouch, Kevin. Don't press on it!" Cathy felt as though she were going to faint from the pain. She took deep breaths to avoid passing out.

"What are we going to do now?" Lillian looked at Kevin, who just shrugged his shoulders helplessly.

"Ask me something easier," he answered softly, while he looked pensively at Cathy. However, his thoughts were with Ricki. *Was she in trouble? What was wrong with the horse that was lying on the ground?*

Cathy seemed to guess what he was thinking.

"You two have to go and take care of Ricki," she said, wincing in pain, and leaned back with her eyes closed tightly.

"We can't just leave you lying here," countered Lillian, but Cathy just nodded weakly.

"Go! Ricki needs you more than I do right now!"
Kevin looked at the uneven path between the boulders and thought it over. "I think it would be possible to get there with the horses," he said slowly.

"Then let's do this: Cathy stays here and we'll go back to

Gwen as fast as possible. Then you and she could ride to Ricki and I'll get Rashid and lead him here and pick up Cathy. I think I can get her into the saddle somehow," said Lillian, determined. She patted her girlfriend on the shoulder encouragingly before she stood up. "It'll be all right. The main thing is not to move even an inch. We don't want you to slip again, and I need to be able to find you."

Cathy tried to smile. "You can be sure that I won't be doing any hiking," she answered, and stifled another cry of pain.

"Good!" said Kevin. "Then let's get going. Come on, Lillian, let's not lose any more time. It'll be dark in a few hours and at some point we have to ride back to the estate." Kevin waved good-bye to Cathy and started off with Lillian.

About fifteen minutes later, they finally returned to an anxious Gwen.

"What took you so long? I was beginning to worry. Who screamed? Where's Cathy? Did something happen to her? I –" Gwendolyn's voice almost broke.

"Don't get upset, Gwen. Cathy slipped and has probably sprained her ankle badly, but otherwise she's okay."

"Thank goodness, but why didn't you bring her back with you?"

"I thought it would be better if I rode back with Holli and Rashid to pick her up. She can't walk," explained Lillian. Then she swung into her saddle and took Rashid's reins out of Gwen's hands.

"You can't ride into the cliffs! That's much too dangerous," began the sixteen-year-old. But Lillian shook her head firmly. "Don't worry, we checked the trail on the way back down. It looks safe enough for the horses."

Gwendolyn shut her eyes in exasperation, gave Sharazan back to his owner, and then mounted her horse. "Okay, I hope you're right! Let's get going!"

"Gwen, we discovered Ricki and Diablo on the other side of the cliffs, and it looked as though a horse was lying out on a ledge. Do you know how to get there?"

Gwen stared at Kevin in disbelief. What he'd just told her couldn't be true!

"Are you sure you saw Ricki and her horse? That's impossible; she's back at the estate in bed! And why would a horse be lying there? That doesn't make sense! You must be mistaken."

"Listen to me. Do you know where the ledge is, or do I have to look for it myself?" From the tone of irritation in Kevin's voice, Gwendolyn could tell he wasn't joking.

"There's only one cliff plateau on the other side. I was there once, but –"

"Then what are we waiting for?" asked Kevin fiercely, and swung himself into Sharazan's saddle.

"Good luck," Lillian wished them and urged Holli forward, back to where Cathy was waiting, leading Rashid, to bring up the rear.

"You, too," replied Kevin. "Let's go, Gwen."

For a moment, she had to fight the urge to hesitate, but then she emphatically complied. "Okay! If it's really like you said, we don't want to lose any time. Come on. We'd better ride around the cliffs. It's longer, but we can gallop once we reach the meadow and it'll be faster in the long run," she said and gracefully turned Black Jack on his hind legs. "Let's go! I have a feeling we'd better hurry."

They gave their horses their heads and started to gallop along the base of the cliffs.

It would have been wonderful to be able to enjoy this ride, thought Kevin. However, considering what might be waiting for them, it was necessary to gallop in order to get there as soon as possible.

Gwendolyn, on the other hand, was less worried about Ricki and Diablo. She was thinking of the horse lying on the ground that Kevin had talked about. Which animal was it? Was it dead? Or sick? She tried to push such thoughts away. It was probably nothing serious – at least that's what she was hoping.

*

William and Hudson had already combed the area for half an hour with no success when they met up with the grooms and Jim, the stable hand.

"What are you two doing here?" asked Mario, perplexed, when he recognized the two house employees.

"Probably the same thing you're doing!" answered William seriously.

"Her Highness is furious because that sick girl and her black horse have disappeared, Sunshine is not in her stall, and none of you could be found anywhere," added Hudson angrily. He was still mad, because he would have preferred to spend his free time with Martha rather than traipse around the countryside looking for lost people and animals.

"What? That girl and her horse are missing, too? That's just great! Everything is going wrong today. Do you have any idea where she could be?" Jim looked back and forth between Hudson and William, but both of them just shook their heads.

"Would we be driving around out here if we did? Where's Sunshine?" asked William.

"Your guess is as good as mine," Chester shrugged. "The mare disappeared from the south pasture."

"I'd have thought that, being so close to term, she wouldn't be able to go anywhere," Mario supported his friend.

"We've looked everywhere we could think of, but the animal is just nowhere to be found," said Jim.

"Have you searched the cliffs?" asked William.

Chester shook his head. "She can't possibly be there. I can't imagine she could get that far in her condition."

"I don't think so either. We need to search systematically all around the farm. I'm almost certain that she's somewhere really close by." Mario looked around at the others and waited for their approval.

"I think so, too!" Chester went back to the Jeep. "Let's hope that she turns up safe and sound and that we find that girl and her horse quickly."

William nodded. "This weekend has been jinxed right from the beginning," he added, and then the men separated to try their luck again.

*

Ricki had almost reached the mare. She stared at the horse, as though her eyes could force it to remain lying on the ground. Sunshine let herself fall back on her side with a loud groan. She lay still for a few seconds, but her frightened heavy breathing and the waves of labor pains caused her body to spasm and tremble.

The poor animal was completely exhausted, and it

seemed doubtful that she had enough energy left to push her foal out of her body.

Ricki took advantage of Sunshine's exhaustion and arrived at her head in two or three steps. She took hold of the bridle with one hand and stroked the animal cautiously with the other.

"Good girl, you are being soooo gooood. Stay calm, sweetie, you don't need to be afraid. I won't disturb you, but you have to stay on the ground, do you hear me? You just can't get up. I read somewhere that if you do, the foal could slip out of place, or your labor could stop, and then the foal would suffocate. You don't want that to happen, do you, my good girl?"

Ricki gently stroked a few strands of mane away from the mare's sweaty forehead.

Sunshine stared at her with huge eyes. The animal didn't know yet what to expect from this person she'd never seen before. But Ricki's friendly voice calmed Sunshine a bit and slowly she began to breathe a little more regularly. But when she heard the sound of hooves, when Diablo came up closer, you could see the whites of her eyes. She laid her ears back and stretched her lips back over her teeth to show her anger and fear of the strange black horse. Clearly, she didn't want him around now.

"Diablo! Stand still! Do you hear me? Stay where you are! Right now!" Ricki's firm voice made the gelding jerk, and he stood motionless and looked at her suspiciously. He felt jealous that Ricki was paying attention to the mare lying on the ground... and ignoring him, except to shout at him and to tell him to stand still. Angrily he snorted and took another step forward, which made the mare very unhappy.

With great effort she whinnied a warning and got up on her front legs in an attempt to stand up.

Ricki hung on to the bridle in panic and tried to hold the animal down, but the harder she tried, the stronger Sunshine seemed resist. The mare swung her head angrily to the side and Ricki was forced to let go.

"Sunshine, stop it! she screamed in panic. "Diablo won't hurt you. Good grief, please lie still. Diablo, you stand still! Still! Ouch!"

Ricki jumped two steps away to get out of the mare's reach, but not fast enough. In fear and anger, Sunshine had snapped at the girl and had bitten her in the lower arm. It wasn't serious, but it was painful.

While the girl pressed her hand over the wound with tears in her eyes, the mare had actually managed to get up awkwardly.

Panting heavily, Sunshine turned around and tried to size up Diablo, who she thought was her enemy, and Ricki noticed with concern that the hooves of the foal had slipped outside again and even a bit of its head was now visible.

"NO!"

Diablo played his ears back and forth but he continued to stand as still as a statue.

Sunshine went toward him on shaky legs, not letting him out of her sight for a second. She believed this big black horse was out to harm her and her foal, and she wasn't going to let him near.

Ricki held her breath.

The foal, she thought. *I can't let it suffocate. I just hope Diablo doesn't do anything stupid right now. Oh, why couldn't the mare just stay where she was?*

At that moment it happened: Sunshine screamed horribly and went after Diablo with her teeth.

The black horse, who hadn't reckoned on this attack, whinnied back furiously. Threateningly, he reared up on his hind legs and struck out at the pregnant mare.

Sunshine saw the kicking hooves in front of her, but because of her condition and her exhaustion, she wasn't able to get far enough away, and Diablo hit her on the croup painfully before he set down on the ground again.

Sunshine bent down under Diablo's weight and sank to the ground.

Diablo wanted to rear up and attack the mare again, but he stopped abruptly when he heard Ricki shout harshly at him in a tone of voice he had never heard his owner use before.

Frightened, but also bewildered, he looked at the girl who was running toward him to grab onto his bridle. Before she could grab hold of him, he jumped to the side, and with a last, and as it seemed to Ricki, incredibly insulted look, the gelding turned away and raced back over the trail he had come at a dangerous speed.

Ricki's knees gave way. She fell to the ground sobbing bitterly and covered her eyes with her hands. Her conscience tormented her: *It's all YOUR fault. YOU'RE to blame if the mare is injured. YOU brought Diablo here and didn't even tie him up! YOU are to blame if the foal suffocates because the mare interrupted her birthing process in panic. It's YOUR fault if something happens to Diablo because YOU didn't take care of him!*

*

77

Carefully Lillian let Doc Holliday go forward, while Rashid trotted obediently behind him on a long lead.

It wasn't as easy to manage this trail as Lillian had imagined, especially leading another horse. Cautiously she checked out every inch of trail that lay ahead, so that the animals wouldn't stumble, and she was relieved when she reached the place where the trail widened. It wasn't very far from where Cathy was waiting.

"We've almost made it," Lillian sighed with relief and glanced gratefully at the two nimble horses. However, she wouldn't really be happy until she had left the cliff area with Cathy safe in the saddle.

"You got back quickly," her girlfriend greeted Lillian gratefully. "I thought it would take much longer. Did Kevin and Gwen ride over to Ricki?"

Lillian nodded yes and jumped down from the saddle.

"At least that's where they were headed," she answered. "How are you? Are you still in a lot of pain?"

"Hmm, if I don't move, I don't feel a thing, but if I put any weight on the foot, I can hear the angels singing." At least Cathy hadn't lost her sense of humor, and Lillian was glad about that.

"Well, let's see if we can get you onto Rashid without causing the heavenly hosts to rejoice," she said and took both sets of reins in one hand. She held her other hand out to Cathy in order to help her up.

Cathy grimaced but she tried not to groan.

"Good," said Lillian. "Now's the difficult part. You have to come over to me, and hop in between Holli and Rashid, so that I can help you. Does your knee hurt, too?"

Cathy shook her head no and supported herself awkwardly on Rashid's neck in order to get to the desired spot.

"Great! Then you can bend it so that I can give you some leverage."

Cathy leaned against the saddle and nodded. Cautiously she bent her leg, and Lillian shoved her hand under the knee.

"At the count of three, okay?"

Her girlfriend nodded and prepared herself for the pain that would come.

"Ready? So... one... two... threeee... " Lillian pushed Cathy upward, and the girl cried out in pain, in spite of her good intentions.

Rashid and Holli were a little spooked, but Lillian held on to them tightly and felt great relief as Cathy finally sat in the saddle.

Tears ran down the injured girl's cheeks, but she laughed anyway. "That really hurts! Man, I'm glad that's over, but I'm not going to put my foot in the stirrup!"

"Do you want me to lead Rashid, or can you manage without using your legs?" Lillian asked as she mounted up.

"Thanks a lot, but Rashid reacts well to the reins."

"Okay. I'll be glad when we've made it back."

Cathy nodded. "Me, too. I've decided that sometimes it's better to listen to others than to always try to get your own way."

Lillian didn't respond, but she knew her friend was right. At the moment she had to concentrate on the trail. She wanted no more missteps.

*

Hudson became increasingly impatient, and started to complain all the time. That made William so angry that he rolled his eyes and wondered why he hadn't left Hudson behind at the estate.

"Look, let me make a suggestion," offered William. "I have a feeling that we're not going to find the girl or the missing horses around here. Let's drive to the cliffs. Something tells me we'll have more luck there."

Hudson looked up at the sky. "Don't you think that Chester and Mario know the horses better than we do? If both of them say that the mare can't walk that far, then that's probably true, right?"

"NO! I don't think so!" countered William, exasperated. "The only thing that I have learned in the past hour and a half is that no one is around here. We're going to the cliffs, and if we don't have any luck there either, we'll drive back home. Then you can take care of Her Highness and I can take off alone. Okay?"

Hudson grumbled and mumbled something unintelligible to William, but at least he turned the car around and drove in the direction William wanted.

Finally! William thought to himself, keeping a close watch out of the car window.

After a while, the cliffs appeared in the distance, and William sat up straight in the passenger seat. He let his eyes swing slowly around, and then suddenly, he grabbed Hudson's arm.

"Hey, do you want me to drive into a ditch? Why did you scare me like that?"

William pointed through the glass excitedly. "Over there! Up ahead! There are two riders galloping like crazy. Don't you see them?"

"So? I thought that we were looking for a pregnant mare and –"

80

"Step on the gas! Maybe the two of them have seen the horse. Should I take over?"

"I've been asking myself the whole time why I have to drive *you* around when *you're* the chauffeur!"

William didn't feel like fighting with Hudson, so he remained silent. He kept staring at the two riders in the distance, who had just ridden around a cliff and disappeared out of his sight.

*

Ricki couldn't seem to hear or see anything anymore. She wept uncontrollably, unable to get up. But the mare's groans of pain brought her back to reality.

One last time, she looked down the trail where Diablo had gone, but she couldn't see any trace of her beloved horse.

Slowly the girl stood up and worked her way over to Sunshine, who was looking trustingly at her.

"I'm so sorry," Ricki whispered softly. "I never wanted anything to happen to you... or to your foal. Diablo – you know, actually, he's very sweet, but in your condition you were afraid of him, of course, and that's why you attacked him. Sunshine, please forgive me."

The spasms in the horse's belly were more violent than ever and the labor set in again.

Ricki held her breath as the mare began to push her foal out, but with each contraction the foal slipped only a fraction of an inch.

The girl stood tensely behind Sunshine and tried to remember what she had read about the birth of a foal in her riding magazine a few days before, but she couldn't recall a thing. It was like when she had to take a test at school. Even though she had studied and prepared and knew a lot about the topic, when the exam paper was in front of her on the desk, she couldn't remember a thing.

"Total blackout," she used to say in her defense, when her grades weren't as good as she had thought they would be.

Strong contractions coursed through the horse's body in waves, but Sunshine wasn't able to push with each one. She was too exhausted from the previous exertions.

Ricki shifted her weight from one leg to the other. *The foal is suffocating in her body and it's your fault!* hammered in her brain. She pressed her hands against her forehead in desperation. The thought that the foal would not be born alive almost tore her heart out.

"Oh, please, God, let it live! Sunshine, please, hang in there, you'll make it... and your baby will too, I'm sure of it!"

Ricki kept talking softly and encouragingly to the mare, but she wasn't really convinced that this birth was going to end well.

And once again a contraction came and the mare was able to push.

Ricki had no idea how long this procedure, which was very painful for the mare, could last.

"I can't just pull on the foal's legs," she said quietly to herself. "But I hate just standing around watching and seeing that the labor isn't progressing well... Oh, why doesn't someone come who knows something about it?"

Sunshine bore down and pushed again at that moment and the foal slid out a little bit more, coming closer to being born.

"Good girl, Sunshine. You're doing really really well!" praised Ricki in a shaky voice. "Don't give up. I'm sure you'll be done soon."

*

"So, if I remember right, we have to turn there onto the narrow path between the boulders and that will lead us directly onto the ledge." Gwendolyn had reined in her horse Black Jack and pointed now to the narrow corridor that would supposedly bring the two riders to Ricki.

"That's great!" Kevin glanced gratefully at his companion and then pressed his legs against Sharazan's belly to urge him on.

"Wait! Stop!" Gwen turned pale and looked past the boy.

"What's wrong?" Kevin asked, turning around to look, and was shocked to see Diablo galloping as though chased by wolves!

"Diablo! Why is he running loose without Ricki? Where is she?"

Sharazan whinnied a friendly greeting as he recognized his stable companion, but the black horse just raced onward, never stopping.

Kevin felt conflicted. On the one hand, he was very worried about Ricki and wanted to get to her quickly, but on the other hand, he couldn't just stand by watching Diablo run away.

Gwendolyn made the decision for him.

"Catch him!" called Gwen. "You have a better chance than I do because he knows you! I'll ride to the ledge and see what's going on there. Okay?"

Without waiting for Kevin's answer, she urged Black

Jack forward, and Kevin had no choice but to chase after his girlfriend's horse.

Diablo seemed to be galloping faster and faster, and Sharazan would have to really exert himself to keep the distance from becoming insurmountable.

I hope he doesn't step on the reins, thought Kevin, worried, as the wind made his eyes water. *If he falls at this speed* – No, he couldn't bear even to think about it.

Chapter 6

"What's going on?" William wondered out loud, turning to Hudson, whose face was becoming darker with annoyance by the minute.

"Can't you tell? They're having a race! Back and forth. This is crazy!" Hudson mumbled as he observed what was happening before their eyes.

"Crazy is what you're talking!" responded William angrily. "Can't you see that one of the horses doesn't have a rider? Something must have happened! Hurry up, cut him off!"

"You can't possibly think that I'm going to drive Mrs. Highland's new Rolls-Royce across this field!" Hudson slowed down intentionally.

"Okay, you're right!" William's voice was almost toneless. "Could you stop for a minute?"

Hudson grinned and stepped on the brakes. "You drank too much coffee, didn't you?"

William nodded, got out and walked around the car. On the driver's side, he opened the door and pulled out Hudson, who was bewildered.

"Hey, what's going on –?" asked the astonished butler.

William, his jaw set in anger, got in and slammed the door. "You have two choices," he said. "Either you get in the passenger's seat and sit quietly, or you walk back to the farm and explain to Her High and Mighty Highness that you don't care about her guests or her pregnant mare. And I don't have to tell you what that would mean, do I?"

Hudson shook his head in disbelief. He had never heard William speak so rudely to anyone. "Are you crazy?"

"Okay, then walk!" William got into the driver's seat, started the car, stepped on the gas, and raced across the meadow that was bordered by the road. He had to stop that animal.

*

Kevin saw the car heading straight for Diablo and held his breath, horrified.

"Darn it, who is that? He must be out of his mind!"

Just to be on the safe side, the boy tightened his hold on Sharazan with the reins while Ricki's horse continued racing forward without reacting to the car coming directly at him.

William took his foot off of the gas pedal and held his breath. It looked as though Diablo was not about to change direction.

That horse is crazy! William thought. *Any other animal would have changed his direction, but he* – The man had no choice but to stop the car so as not to collide with the black horse.

"That's Diablo," William realized, his eyes wide in astonishment. "If he's running around here saddled, that can only mean he's thrown his rider." But who could the rider have been? Ricki or Gwen? In either case, he could only imagine how Mrs. Highland would react. And it wouldn't be good.

Diablo raced directly toward the front of the car as though he didn't even see it. William jumped out of the driver's seat onto the field and stood in front of the car waving his arms above his head.

"Diablo! No!" he shouted at the horse, who, seconds later, thundered past him, missing him by inches.

Kevin galloped over to William on Sharazan and was relieved when he recognized the driver. "Oh man, I am sooooo glad it's you! I thought it –"

"Where's Diablo's rider?" William demanded to know.

"Ricki must be on the ledge. We saw her there from a distance with Diablo and another horse, who was lying on the ground. Gwen is on her way to her and I followed Diablo. I have no idea why he took off."

"A horse is lying on the ground? Is it Sunshine?"

Kevin looked at the driver blankly. "Who's Sunshine?"

"She's Mrs. Highland's very pregnant favorite mare. She got out of the paddock and we've all been out looking for her."

"In that case, she could be giving birth to the foal on the ledge. I don't envy Ricki right now."

"Sunshine is much worse off!" William watched Diablo galloping off in the distance. "Ride after him so that we don't lose him, too. I'll call Mario and Chester on the cell phone. The two of them need to get here as quickly as possible. Then I'll drive back to the farm and get the horse trailer. Somehow, we have to get Sunshine, and maybe her foal, and Diablo back there."

Kevin nodded and instantly resumed chasing Diablo,

while William bumped back across the field in the car and picked up Hudson, who was in a foul mood.

"Get in, and don't say a word!" he snapped at the butler in a warning tone, and then he stepped on the gas.

*

In the meantime, Lillian and Cathy had left the trail between the boulders with their horses and were glad that they had firm ground under the horses' hooves again.

"How's your ankle?" Lillian asked for the umpteenth time.

Cathy had to laugh, despite the pulsing pain. "It's still connected! Thanks for asking. Walking back would have been much worse," she said thankfully and patted Rashid's neck.

"Then let's ride back to the estate, okay?"

"And Ricki? I'd really love to know what's wrong with that horse on the ground," countered Cathy.

"Don't tell me you still haven't had enough? Someone should look at your ankle –"

"Oh, c'mon, Lillian, it can't swell up any worse than it already is, and they'll probably have to cut off the boot to get to it. And anyway, I don't have to walk on it! Rashid does it –"

"Cathy, you are impossible! Why not just tell me you want to ride after Gwen and Kevin!" grinned Lillian.

"Exactly!" answered Cathy simply, and guided her dun horse in the other direction.

Just then, Diablo practically flew around the cliff and almost collided with Doc Holliday, who jumped to the side, frightened, and almost threw Lillian from the saddle.

Ricki's horse had to come to a full stop, and he halted just in front of Rashid.

Cathy bent down and reached for the reins of the runaway horse. "Diablo, what are *you* doing here? Where's Ricki?"

Diablo's nostrils flared and his flanks trembled. He stood on shaky legs and breathed heavily.

"What now?" Cathy glanced questioningly at Lillian. "Should we take Diablo back or go find Ricki?"

"Ricki," the older girl decided quickly. "After all, she has to get back home, too." She rode around Diablo and took his reins from Cathy.

"Just make sure that you stay in the saddle. I'm used to leading horses by now," she added, and then both girls rode off to find Ricki.

After they'd gone a few yards, Kevin came rushing toward them on Sharazan, When he saw that Lillian had Diablo under control and that Cathy sat on Rashid, he reined in Sharazan.

"Thank God," he exclaimed. "At least one less worry!"

*

Frightened, Ricki felt cold sweat run over her body, making her clothes stick to her skin. She was so caught up in her fears for the foal, she didn't even notice her own dizziness.

It seemed to her that the foal had been lodged inside the body of the mare much too long. The contractions were coming one after the other now, and almost the entire head of the little foal was already visible.

Ricki tried to encourage the mare to push, but after a few

89

more minutes, she grew quiet. She realized she was breathing in rhythm with the mare, as though she could help her and support her by doing that. Then, all of a sudden, the foal slid a little farther along the birth canal until its front legs just touched the ground.

"Good, Sunshine!" You're the best!" whispered Ricki as she stared at the foal still encased in the amniotic sac.

Nervously, the girl wrung her hands. She felt that she should do something, but was afraid that she would do something wrong. If only she could recall what she'd read about a horse's birthing process!

Suddenly she remembered! "The sac! I have to open the sac!" Ricki said excitedly as she knelt beside the foal. For a split second she hesitated, but then she grabbed the thin membrane which formed the casing that had protected the foal in his mother's belly for almost a year, and ripped it open above the head and pulled it back a bit. She wiped some mucus from the foal's nose and mouth with the clean cotton handkerchief she had in the pocket of her jeans. But while doing so, she also remembered reading that in order to prevent the foal from taking in germs with its first breaths one should always wear sterile gloves when assisting in the birth.

Oh, sure, Ricki said to herself, *that's fine if you're in a stable with everything you need close by. But here, when you have to improvise, it's better to wipe off his nostrils with a clean handkerchief than to watch the little guy suffocate!*

Sunshine was completely exhausted and made no further attempt to get on with the birthing process. Groaning, she just endured the labor pains, and the foal didn't move an inch.

It's not breathing! thought Ricki, horrified. She could feel the fear constricting her throat. She tried desperately to remember when the article said the lungs of a new born foal start to function on their own.

"The rib cage," she whispered excitedly and swallowed hard. "The rib cage has to be outside; otherwise the lungs won't work! C'mon Sunshine, you have to help me. Please. It's such a beautiful foal. His coat is as shiny as a... a golden star. And it's your child! You can't just give up, Sunshine, your foal is meant to live. Do you hear me?"

A new contraction ran through the mare's body, and after a final, worried look at Sunshine, Ricki knew what she had to do.

Carefully she took hold of the foal's two long front legs and pulled slowly, in the rhythm of the contraction that followed, bit by bit, moving the animal far enough out of the birth canal so that the rib cage was on the ground as well. She tried very hard to pull the foal straight ahead.

After the first half of the little foal was outside Sunshine's body, the contractions subsided momentarily, and Ricki could feel the mare relax some.

"Come on," she begged the foal. "Breathe! You have to breathe!" But the narrow rib cage didn't budge.

"Darn it, you can't do this to me. First I free you from the sac, and then I pull you out. And now you won't breathe. That's... that's not fair of you."

The teenager felt the tears roll down her cheeks again. Had she done something wrong, made a mistake? Had she killed this wonderful creature by intervening?

In despair, she turned her head away and with eyes filled with tears looked at the wide-open beautiful valley that surrounded the cliffs. As she glanced upward she noticed the evening star, which was already visible, although the sun hadn't set yet.

What had she said a while ago? A coat that shone like a golden star...

Ricki turned back toward the foal and whispered: "Live, Golden Star. You must live!"

*

Gwendolyn had almost reached the end of the path on Black Jack and could see the ledge in front of her. Her heart seemed to stop as she immediately recognized her favorite mare. A few seconds later she realized that Ricki was kneeling behind Sunshine.

"What on earth is Sunshine doing here? I thought she was safe and sound in her stall? The foal –" Gwendolyn whispered hoarsely and her knees started to shake. "Sunshine is having her foal and Ricki – My God, what is she doing there? Does she know anything about foaling? This can't be happening."

Keeping her wits about her, she halted Black Jack so that the mare wouldn't become frightened. Then she quickly looked around but couldn't find anything to tie her horse to. She had no choice but to stay put, although she would have much preferred to comfort Sunshine and greet the new foal. Oddly, at the moment, she wasn't thinking of Ricki at all.

"It looks like the foal is just about there," she whispered to Black Jack, and put her hand across his muzzle to stop him from whinnying.

"Shhh," she said softly. "Stay calm. The last thing Sunshine and her foal need now is any excitement!"

*

Mario and Chester arrived at the cliffs about the same time as Lillian, Cathy, and Kevin.

"Where did you guys come from?" Chester asked as the Jeep came to a halt. He leaped out of the front seat in order to get to Sunshine as quickly as possible, in case William had been right that the mare was around here somewhere and probably foaling.

"We'll tell you later!" answered Kevin, who could tell that Chester didn't want to lose any time. Mario, too, just nodded briefly at the teens before he ran off after Chester.

"And don't even think about riding after us!" yelled Chester over his shoulder. "If Sunshine really is having her foal, you would only disturb the birthing process by being there, is that clear?"

He was relieved to hear the three teenagers answer, "Okay."

As the two men disappeared out of sight, Lillian and Kevin dismounted, while Cathy stayed in the saddle because of her injured leg.

"Darn it! Now we don't know any more than we did before!" Kevin exclaimed somewhat annoyed but also worried.

When he thought about Ricki he had a funny feeling in his gut. After all, there had to be a plausible reason for Diablo to have bolted like he did.

"Well, at least Ricki is getting some support," said Cathy, and Lillian added: "Yeah, support, but with what? Do you guys really think it's Sunshine lying back there? If you ask me, that's impossible."

"Nothing's impossible!" responded Kevin and stared at

the space between the boulders, as though that would somehow make his girlfriend appear.

"Ricki's probably scared to death about Diablo," said Cathy, and leaned on Rashid's mane. "I'm so glad we were able to catch him."

Kevin nodded exuberantly. "Me, too! You can't imagine how worried I was chasing him, especially when William came toward us in the car! That's something I don't need to experience every day. And who knew Diablo's such a race-horse? Wow, it was really awesome, how fast he was!"

"I'm worried about the other horse," said Cathy. "It doesn't matter if it's Sunshine or not, I would give anything to know what's happening back there."

*

"If anything has happened to that girl or to Sunshine, you're all fired!" Eleanor Highland screamed at her chauffeur, bouncing back and forth on the passenger seat of the horse trailer.

William exhaled loudly. Slowly but surely, his employer's bad temper was starting to get on his nerves. She had been in a foul mood all day, and William had the impression that she was letting all of her anger out on him, even though none of what happened today was his fault.

"Come on, step on the gas! If I need a car-park attendant, I'll hire one!" Mrs. Highland continued her rampage.

William had had enough. It was time to make Mrs. Charles Osgood Highland III aware of the unfairness of her accusations and her mistreatment of others.

He let the car roll to a stop and shut off the motor.

Completely baffled by the sudden stop, the owner of

Highland Farms turned toward her chauffeur, her face bright red with rage. "That is absolutely incredible! You are –"

"Excuse me," William said coolly, putting up his hand to silence her in mid-sentence. He tried to remain calm. "But the way you treat your employees is just as incredible! Today, and a lot of other days, your behavior towards us is the pits. Since you want to fire all of us anyway, I might as well say it; you have no right to belittle and bully the people who work for you.

"Well, that is just not –" The lady was getting very upset, but William was determined to have his say.

"I'm not finished yet! All of us work very hard every day, but all we ever hear from you is what we haven't finished yet and what we should be doing when we're doing something else. In case you haven't noticed, we only have two hands, like other people, and we would appreciate being treated with dignity and respect, and not like your slaves! And just so you know why we all haven't quit yet: We love the horses, the farm, and the countryside here. But most of all, we're all very fond of Gwen, who always manages to smooth over your insults and meanness with her sweet disposition and her sense of justice. *That's* why we're still here."

William paused briefly before adding: "So now you can fire me and chauffeur yourself around. You've threatened to fire me for less!"

Eleanor Highland sat in stunned silence following William's long speech. After what seemed like an eternity, she began to nod slowly, tears filling her eyes.

"Am I really such a monster?" she asked, her voice breaking, while she looked William straight in the eyes.

95

The chauffeur exhaled deeply and managed a slight smile. "Even worse!" he answered, and she understood.

"All right. Would you please take the monster to her pregnant mare? My failures aren't the horse's fault –" She stared at her chauffeur and waited for his response, but he stared right back and showed no reaction at all.

"You've got courage, William," said Eleanor Highland after a long pause. "I've always liked that about you. You're not afraid of the consequences, and you always speak your mind. You remind me of my late husband. William, I'd like to apologize to you formally. I wasn't aware that I was treating you all so shabbily. It's time that I take my grand-daughter as a model for my behavior, don't you think?"

She smiled at her driver almost shyly. "Would it be all right if I asked you to help me in this process of rethinking my life? After all, I'll need someone to keep me in line, to keep me from slipping back into my old habits, don't you think?"

William looked at her thoughtfully for a moment, and then he held out his hand to her. "Under one condition," he said.

"And what would that be?"

"Hudson and Martha were going to spend their night off together. The current situation means that's out of the question. I want you to let them make up for it tomorrow."

"They're in love, aren't they?" Mrs. Highland asked as understanding dawned, and William just grinned.

"I promise!" She shook his hand, and then William started the trailer and drove toward the cliffs.

"Thank you for your honesty," Eleanor Highland said softly and pressed William's arm.

Sunshine had gathered all of her remaining strength and pushed so hard that Ricki was afraid the mare would hurt herself. The front half of the foal lay crumpled on the ground.

Ricki thought she remembered reading that this position was supposed to make the birth easier for the mare and the foal, since the rest of the foal could now move more easily through the birth canal. However, it looked as though Sunshine had used up all of her strength by pushing with the last contraction, and now she lay still, completely exhausted.

The girl realized that she would have to help the animal one more time, so she reached for the foal's long, thin, little legs.

The next two contractions were enough to allow Golden Star, as Ricki had baptized the little foal in her mind, to slide out of its mother's body.

The hind legs were still encased in the amniotic sac and the little creature lay folded up behind its mother.

Ricki stared hopelessly at the soaking wet mare and the motionless foal.

Feverishly, she tried to remember what she could do to make the foal begin breathing, but she had absolutely no idea how to resuscitate a horse.

I wonder if it's the same as mouth to mouth resuscitation of a person? she asked herself, but just then she thought she noticed the slightest trace of a movement of the foal's tiny rib cage.

"Please... please," she whispered again, placing her hand carefully on the foal's coat. Right away, the little nostrils filled up with air, and Golden Star shook his head lightly. Ricki suppressed a yell of excitement and happiness. Laughing and crying at the same time, she tried to keep herself from hugging the wonderful creature that lay before her.

"Welcome to the world," she stammered, deeply moved. "You are the most beautiful foal I've ever seen. Congratulations, Sunshine. You're the best."

*

Chester and Mario finally arrived at the place where Gwendolyn stood with Black Jack watching the birth breathlessly.

She jumped as she suddenly noticed the two men behind her.

"What are you doing here?" asked Mario, perplexed. Without a word, Gwen pointed up ahead.

"Darn it, I didn't really believe that we would find Sunshine here! Gwen, you have to go back home immediately with Black Jack!"

"But –"

"No buts! We can't take the risk of your gelding frightening the mare."

"I –" Gwendolyn tried again to protest that she didn't want to leave now, but Mario wouldn't budge.

"Gwen, I said now! Do you understand me?"

Sighing, the girl looked down before she awkwardly turned her horse around.

"Without Ricki, Sunshine would have been a goner," she whispered to the men quietly. "She pulled the foal out, and she –"

"She did what?" Chester and Mario both turned pale. They were thinking the same thing. Hopefully, the mare hadn't been injured by Ricki's amateur attentions.

"Don't worry, just go now," repeated Mario as he gently pushed Gwendolyn away.

"I'm not worried!" the teenager said pointedly, and threw Ricki another glance over her shoulder.

Ricki had been so absorbed with the foal that she hadn't noticed that Gwen had been watching her all that time and that the two stable grooms had arrived. A huge weight dropped from Ricki's shoulders when she saw the two men hurrying toward her with comforting words for the mare.

On shaky legs, she stumbled over to the wall of the cliff and leaned against it. She replayed the last few minutes in her mind, when she had been so worried that the foal wouldn't live.

She watched Chester take care of the foal and Mario look after the mare. Sunshine was already trying to get up.

"It's a wonderful male foal," said Chester, beaming his pleasure. "It looks like both the mother and the foal are okay! Great job, nurse! Congratulations on helping with the birth – Ricki? Where'd she go?"

Bewildered, the groom looked all around, but the girl had vanished.

*

Completely numb from this amazing experience, Ricki suddenly became very sad. She remembered that Diablo had bolted. Worrying about the foal hadn't given her time to think about anything else, but now her concern for Diablo had taken over.

99

She ran so quickly along the path she thought her lungs would burst from the exertion.

If anything has happened to Diablo, I won't be able to stand it, she thought, and she wished at that moment that she and her horse had never come to Highland Farms.

Chapter 7

Returning from the cliffs, Gwendolyn was pleasantly surprised to see her other three guests, with Cathy astride Rashid, and Diablo in tow.

"Boy, am I relieved to see that you've caught Ricki's horse. Cathy, are you okay?"

"I could be worse!"

"Hey, what's going on out on the ledge? Mario and Chester wouldn't let us ride over there!" Kevin was almost bursting with worry for Ricki, but also from curiosity. Gwendolyn waved away his anxiety and slid down from Black Jack's saddle.

"Everything's fine! You have no idea what Ricki managed to do! All I can say is, my hat's off to her! Your girlfriend is amazing!" Gwendolyn shook her head in admiration, but Lillian nudged her with her elbow.

"C'mon, Gwen, tell us, already! Explain!"

Gwendolyn looked at three pairs of eyes, all staring at her in anticipation, and when she finally began telling them the details, a huge smile spread over her face.

"Sunshine had her foal and Ricki pulled it out. I couldn't believe my eyes, as she... "

*

The friends listened in silent awe as Gwen related the story of the foal's birth and Ricki's part in it, occasionally shaking their heads in disbelief.

"I would have loved to run over to the little fellow and cuddle it," she said, ending her report, "but Chester sent me away because of Black Jack." Grinning, she kissed her gelding on his muzzle and patted his neck. "Luckily, he was there. If I hadn't had him to lean on, I would have fainted, I was so scared!" she laughed easily now, relieved that it was over.

Lillian and Cathy were completely dumbstruck and couldn't utter a word. They knew that Ricki was capable of a lot, but they would never have thought that she would attempt to help with the delivery of a foal.

"Wow," was Kevin's only response. He was so proud of his girlfriend he couldn't get out more than that one word.

Just then, Ricki came running out from the cliffs.

Diablo raised his head, pointed his ears, and whinnied loudly at her.

On hearing the familiar whinny, she stopped abruptly, breathing hard, and stared at her beloved black horse with huge eyes.

"Diablo," she whispered hoarsely, and closed her eyes with joy, only to open them two seconds later to make sure he wasn't a mirage. Not only was her horse still standing there, but all of her friends were there too, standing around him.

As she ran to be reunited with them all, she glanced skyward and whispered a prayer of thanks. The moment she reached Diablo and hugged him was one of the happiest times in her life. She had her horse back, and he was safe and sound. Finally, standing beside her darling Diablo, she could feel completely happy about little Golden Star. His birth was no longer overshadowed by Diablo's disappearance.

Just as Kevin was about to embrace Ricki and tell her how relieved he was that she was all right, William drove up in the horse trailer with Gwendolyn's grandmother.

With a nimble jump that no one would have guessed her capable of, Eleanor Highland got out of the vehicle, her face showing obvious delight and relief at seeing Ricki and her horse standing in front of her.

"Where in the world were you?" she asked Ricki a bit accusingly. But instead of waiting for her answer, she took her granddaughter aside.

"What about Sunshine?" she asked excitedly. And as Gwendolyn pointed to the cliff ledge and shouted happily, "The foal is there! Ricki –" her grandmother gratefully clasped her hands together.

"Thank goodness... You can tell me all about it later!... William, come with me!"

The chauffeur hesitated because of her tone, and Mrs. Highland corrected herself immediately.

"William, would you be so kind as to accompany me? And please take the basket with the two blankets and the towels with you."

The man smiled and nodded approvingly as he opened the trunk. "Of course! No problem!"

Gwendolyn could hardly believe her ears and stared at them both. "What's going on here?" she murmured. She was sure that she hadn't heard right.

The foal had already taken his first few unsteady steps by the time Mrs. Highland and William arrived at the cliff ledge.

Mario held Sunshine, who had turned away from her foal, by her bridle, while Chester tried to help the foal balance himself on his crossed legs.

The sight of the little horse caused Eleanor Highland to stop where she was. Although she'd seen many foals in her life, the sight of a newborn foal always warmed her heart.

"Isn't it marvelous, William?" she asked, looking in wonderment at her animals.

"A strong little man, ma'am," responded Mario softly as he rubbed Sunshine between the ears.

Eleanor Highland smiled. "He does his father, Garibaldi, proud," she replied and came a little closer. "We brought blankets and towels with us." She took the basket out of William's hands and went over to the horses.

Quietly she talked to Sunshine, and the mare whinnied her greeting softly. The little foal was so surprised by his mother's voice that he wobbled and fell down again. But by the next attempt he was standing much more sure of himself, with his legs spread out widely. He whinnied triumphantly.

I made it! he seemed to say to the people around him. Then, instinctively, the little creature started to move on shaky legs toward the udder and, with Chester's help, he finally found the milk source so he could satisfy his first hunger.

Sunshine laid back her ears and tried to bite Mario.

"Huh, what's that about? You never had a problem with

stilling milk. C'mon, put your hoof down! You don't want to hit your baby, do you?"

Chester was glad that he had knotted up the afterbirth so that Sunshine couldn't tear it off with her hooves.

"The mare has to get used to the foal sucking. Isis always makes a big deal out of it, but after the second or third time, everything's fine!" he grinned and shoved the frightened little foal's head back underneath its reluctant mother.

"Don't let her do that, little man! Only the strong survive!"

Hungrily, the foal tried again to grab hold of one of the teats, but Sunshine backed away again. She stepped aside angrily and rolled her eyes menacingly.

"Uh oh," exclaimed Mario. "If she keeps that up, the little guy will starve."

Chester shook his head with concern.

"Up to now, almost every one of our mares has learned how to still, and, after all, this isn't Sunshine's first foal. C'mon, young man, let's give it another try," he encouraged softly. But as soon as the little foal got closer to his mother, Sunshine whinnied shrilly and moved backward, pulling Mario with her.

"Good grief, not one step farther. We don't want you both falling off the ledge," cautioned a nervous Mrs. Highland. Mario was able to stop the mare from stepping back farther only by exerting all of his strength.

Meanwhile Chester held the foal securely in his arms and tried to force him toward his mother.

"This isn't working! I have no idea why Sunshine's acting this way! We may have to feed him ourselves," he shouted.

"Fine! But first we have to get home. William, go get the trailer," ordered Gwendolyn's grandmother, then caught herself and added, "Please."

"I'm afraid that's not possible!"

"What is that supposed to mean: 'that's not possible'?"

"We'll have to lead the horses back through the boulders. It's much too narrow for the trailer," explained William.

The owner of Highland Farms tapped her forehead with her hand.

"Of course! How foolish of me! I've been under a lot of stress today," she admitted, and looked pensively at the foal.

"Well, the poor little thing is much too weak to make it down by himself, and Sunshine doesn't seem interested in helping him. If only I knew why she rejected him!" she said. "In any event, what matters now is how we are going to get him to the vehicle."

Mario and Chester looked at each other. They were both very strong and they knew what was coming.

"Couldn't you carry him?" Mrs. Highland asked politely.

"We could," answered Mario, "but that would be awful for him, since Chester and I would have to take turns a few times, until we –"

"You're right, Mario," the horsewoman said, brushing the idea aside.

William cleared his throat. "Well, I don't know very much about it, but there are five strong horses on the other side of the cliffs. Wouldn't it be possible to lay the little guy across one of their backs and transport him like that? I mean –"

Eleanor Highland looked at Mario and Chester. "Do you think that would work?"

Both men exchanged glances. "I don't see why not!" said Mario.

"Then we'll do it that way!" she decided and turned back to her driver. "William, please go back and send Gwendolyn and Black Jack to me. Tell her what we've decided to do and to hurry. With newborn foals every minute counts!"

William nodded and hurried off immediately, while Mrs. Highland unfolded one blanket after another and placed them over the backs of the mare and foal.

"When you're home, you'll get used to each other," she said softly to the animals. She hoped she was right. But the way things were looking right now, Sunshine didn't want anything to do with her foal.

"Something extremely painful or frightening must have happened either just before or during the birth, which the mare associates with giving birth to her foal," Gwendolyn's grandmother thought aloud. "When we know what caused this behavior, we can work on changing it." However, at the moment, she couldn't imagine what the mare could have gone through.

*

The friends were startled when an out-of-breath William emerged from between the boulders and shouted from a distance: "Gwen, you've got to ride to the ledge on Black Jack immediately! Sunshine won't accept her foal and won't let it nurse. It's too difficult for the foal to come here to the trailer himself. Black Jack is supposed to carry him!"

"What? Oh no! That's impossible!" Gwendolyn said forcefully, shaking her head. "Black Jack will never do it!

Has my grandmother forgotten? He'll only tolerate me on his back. He'd throw off the foal before they'd even let go of him. Isn't there any other way?"

William shook his head. "The path is too narrow. I can't get the trailer through!"

The friends looked at each other in silence. All of a sudden, Ricki threw the reins over Diablo's head and swung herself into the saddle.

"Diablo will carry the little fellow!" she said, completely convinced. "I don't know how he'll react to the situation, but it'll work somehow!" Before the others could say anything, she turned her horse and rode off.

Only after she had ridden some distance did she remember how Diablo and Sunshine had behaved toward one another. Now she wasn't so sure that it was a good idea to ride back on Diablo. However, it was too late to go back. Golden Star needed help desperately, and for the second time that day Ricki was ready to do everything she could for the little guy.

*

Anxiously Eleanor Highland awaited her granddaughter's arrival. With growing unease, she noticed that Sunshine was behaving more and more aggressively toward her foal, who only wanted to drink the first few sips of milk from his mother's udder and to be close to her. He kept whinnying weakly. Sunshine, however, ignored him completely.

"I hope Gwen gets here soon with Black Jack," said Chester as he held the foal tightly in his arms to prevent him from getting hurt.

Finally, the sound of hooves on the stony path could be

heard, and with it a collective sigh of relief from those gathered at the birth site.

"Gwendolyn, I'm so glad you're here – Ricki? What are you doing here? Where's Gwendolyn?" Eleanor Highland looked skeptically at Diablo, who rolled his eyes nervously when he saw Sunshine. He had not forgotten her bite.

"Gwen said that Black Jack wouldn't tolerate anyone or anything on his back except her, but we need to transport the foal on Diablo."

"Child, that is extremely kind of you, but I don't know your horse, and Sunshine's foal is an extremely valuable animal," Gwendolyn's grandmother politely declined the offer.

"But we don't have any other way of getting to the trailer," Mario interjected, and Chester nodded in agreement.

"We should try it anyway!"

"And besides, it shouldn't really matter whether it's a valuable Garibaldi foal or a scraggly pony foal, should it? It's about something completely different, isn't it?" Ricki couldn't keep quiet. It hurt her pride that Mrs. Highland didn't trust Diablo.

"All right, if that's what all of you think. Let's get going. It's time for us to go home; the animal needs nourishment urgently! A foal has to get mother's milk within the first six hours after the birth. There are valuable antibodies in the milk that build up the foal's immune system. Sunshine will have to be milked."

Chester rolled his eyes. Why did their employer feel it necessary to give this speech to her experienced stable hands, who had raised innumerable foals?

"Can we get going?" he urged and was glad when Mrs. Highland finally nodded her consent.

Ricki, who had listened closely to what Mrs. Highland had said, turned to the groom. "What should I do?" she asked eagerly.

Chester explained to her: "First of all, the little guy and your horse have to get to know one another a little bit. Otherwise your Diablo would definitely not be in favor of putting a kicking foal with a strange smell onto his back, unless he has the opportunity to sniff it a while. The best thing to do is to lead him here, slowly, one step at a time, with little pauses, while I calm down the foal. You can see that he's rolling his eyes in fear."

Ricki nodded and tried not to let Diablo sense her excitement.

"Come, my good boy, Golden Star needs your help!" she said quietly, stroking her horse's neck again and again to comfort him.

"Golden Star?" questioned Mrs. Highland, astounded to hear that Ricki had named the foal.

The girl turned red with embarrassment. "Excuse me, I gave him that name... because his coat is so shiny."

"Oh, I see," the foal's owner smiled and then she stepped aside so that she wouldn't be in the way.

Sunshine watched the approaching gelding with her ears laid back. The incident with Diablo was still fresh in her memory. She bared her teeth in warning and then, in an unguarded moment, while Mario was watching the little foal, Sunshine bit him.

The young groom screamed loudly.

The mare had buried her teeth in his arm and it didn't look as if the animal wanted to let go.

Sunshine's eyes shone menacingly, and her teeth retained their grip in Mario's flesh.

110

There was nothing for Mario to do but slap the otherwise gentle mare across the muzzle with the palm of his hand. Nevertheless, several seconds went by before she let go of his arm.

Afterward Sunshine turned aside with a jerk, and then raced toward Diablo and Ricki like a demon.

Mario could hardly think straight because of the burning pain in his arm, but, on the other hand, he was a groom, and glad that Sunshine's placenta had completely dropped fifteen minutes ago. That lessened the chance of any possible internal injuries to the mare in her enraged attack on Diablo.

Ricki held the reins of her horse tightly in her hand and stared at the furious mare who halted in front of them, turned around faster than lightning, and then kicked out violently at Diablo.

Desperately the girl tried to move her gelding to the side and keep him under control, but Diablo was not about to give in. *What was this crazy mare thinking, putting his Ricki in danger?*

Threateningly, the giant gelding reared up on his hind legs, pulling the reins out of Ricki's hand.

"Diablo, no!" Ricki screamed at her horse again, but this time the black horse didn't gallop away insulted. He was prepared to defend himself and Ricki.

*

Mario, who held his injured arm tightly with his good hand, made a move to intervene between the two horses in spite of the pain, but Mrs. Highland's commanding tone made him stop.

"No! Mario! Stand still! That's too dangerous! Ricki, be careful! Step to the side, do you hear me? At once!"

Ricki, who had tried one more time to regain the reins, was startled by Mrs. Highland's loud, warning voice and spun around.

Sunshine reared up behind her wildly and, in her panic, tried to trample the girl and her horse.

Ricki stared at the animal in fear and awe. She couldn't move. Never in her life had she seen a horse in such a frenzy. Only in films did things like this happen.

It's over! The thought flashed through her mind, and she became strangely calm.

Mario reacted quickly. He threw his whole two-hundred-pound weight against Ricki, wrapped his arms around her and rolled with her to the side just before Sunshine's powerful hoof came down on the spot where, seconds earlier, the girl had been standing.

Chester had taken the foal over toward the cliff wall, where Mrs. Highland, her face pale and visibly upset, stared at Ricki, who lay protected underneath Mario's hulking form.

Totally crazed, sensing that her foal suddenly was being taken from her, the mare tried to attack Ricki and Mario again, but Diablo was quicker, and he reared up as a living shield between the enraged mare and the two people lying on the ground.

With bared teeth, his ears laid straight back, and a shrill whinny, he signaled that he was prepared to fight if the mare tried to attack Ricki again. Again and again, he reared straight up in the air and drove the mare back, step by step, by kicking at her with his front hooves.

Eleanor Highland had become aware, incredulously, that

Sunshine was getting nearer and nearer to the edge. "Oh no! This is a nightmare... a bad dream," gasped the woman. Her valuable brood mare was very close to falling over the cliff!

*

"They should have been here a long time ago, don't you guys think?" Gwendolyn kept looking back along the trail, but there was no sign of the others.

"It'll take a while before they can get the foal to lie on Diablo's back, and then they'll have to go very slowly so he doesn't fall off," replied Lillian, but Gwendolyn shook her head thoughtfully.

"I don't know... I don't know. I'm going to go see what's keeping them." The sixteen-year-old gave Black Jack's reins to William. "I'm sorry, my boy, I can't take you with me," she comforted her horse and pressed her face into his thick mane. "You heard what Chester said. We don't want to scare Sunshine, although I don't know what there is about you that could possibly scare her."

Laughing, she waved at the others and started down the trail. But after a few minutes, she began to experience a sinking feeling. The closer to the ledge she got, the more convinced she became that something had gone wrong up there. Otherwise she would have met up with everyone by now.

After a while, during which Gwendolyn ran most of the way, she stepped out between the boulders.

Her heart stopped beating for a second, and her blood seemed to freeze in her veins. It took her less than a second to grasp what was happening: her favorite mare was only steps away from the edge of the cliff, and Diablo was standing in front of her, threateningly.

She couldn't see her grandmother, Chester, or the foal from where she was standing, but she could see Mario, who was just helping Ricki stand up.

"What's going on?" whispered Gwendolyn. She seemed ready to faint.

Mario said something to Ricki and tried to hold onto her arm, but the girl broke loose and shook her head violently. Then she turned around and started walking cautiously toward the two horses.

"Diablo, " Gwendolyn heard Ricki call with a shaky voice. "Diablo, come here, my boy. Come here, to me. No! Don't go any farther! You can't go any farther! Do you hear me?"

That was the moment when Gwendolyn awakened abruptly from her state of shock. Quickly, she started to move.

"Sunshine! SUNSHINE –!" she called loudly, waving excitedly with both arms in order to get the mare's attention. But the animal wouldn't look away from Diablo, who wasn't willing to retreat even one step.

Ricki dared to glance back once over her shoulder and saw Gwen coming closer.

"Gwen! Get back! The animals have become unpredictable!" shouted her grandmother.

The sixteen-year-old took a deep breath, but she ignored her grandmother's shrill warning and kept on going.

Sunshine unpredictable? That can't be true! This sweet, always gentle mare is never mean! Never! thought Gwendolyn. She would probably have been less sure of herself if she'd seen what had just happened. However, she moved across the ledge now completely free of doubt. She was only afraid that Sunshine could stumble and fall down the cliff. Why was Diablo standing in front of her like that? What kind of aggressive horse was he to drive her beloved mare to her death?

A sudden feeling of hatred toward Diablo began to grow in Gwendolyn, and angrily she looked Ricki in the eye as the two teenagers approached one another.

"If Sunshine falls down there, I will never forgive you! Your horse is a... killer!" she snarled at Ricki.

"Are you crazy? The mare bit Mario, kicked at the foal, attacked us, and then Diablo came to my rescue!" replied Ricki.

"Is that true?" Gwen asked defensively.

"YEAH!"

The two girls stood facing each other but never letting the horses out of their sight.

"We have to get them away from here," whispered Gwen, who didn't know what to think anymore.

"Yeah, but how?" Ricki's desperation had grown to the point of near panic, and she was glad that Gwendolyn was there next to her. It gave her some security knowing that she wasn't alone in this situation, because right now Chester was busy with the foal, Mario was injured, and Mrs. Highland... Well, the older woman wasn't much help.

"Listen, I'm going to try something. If the horses react and lose interest in each other, maybe we'll be able to grab them. Okay?" whispered Gwen.

"What are you going to do?" asked Ricki.

"Just wait, and don't be surprised. My idea is simple, but up to now, it's worked to calm down every horse in our stable."

Without paying any more attention to Ricki, Gwendolyn began to walk forward, step by step, and as she walked, she began to sing a children's song.

She's singing! thought Ricki, puzzled. *I can't believe it!* Slowly she followed the sixteen-year-old, whose voice was becoming louder so that the horses would pay attention to her.

Chapter 8

At the sound of Gwendolyn's lilting voice, Sunshine raised her head. Diablo, on the other hand, kept watching the mare intently, so that he'd be ready at any moment to counterattack if necessary.

Cautiously the mare risked a glance again in the direction of the voice she knew and loved so well.

Gwendolyn interrupted the melody and called softly to the animal. "Hello, sweetie, it's me. Do you like my song? I'm singing it just for you, do you hear me?" And then Gwendolyn continued singing.

She has a beautiful voice, Ricki thought, and noticed that even Diablo had begun to steal looks at Gwen from out of the corner of his eyes.

It's working! Ricki was amazed. *Who would have believed it? Oh, Diablo, please don't do anything stupid. Turn around... please, please, turn around!*

Ricki focused her eyes on her horse's head and hoped that he had heard her thoughts and would turn toward her. After all, it worked on people. All you had to do was stare at someone until the person turned around to see who was looking at him. You could feel that kind of look.

At first, when Eleanor Highland heard her granddaughter sing, she thought Gwendolyn had gone crazy. But now, seeing the animals react to the melody, she had hope that things might work out after all.

However, Mario saw it differently. "The two of them are nuts!" he said with a worried shake of his head, but Chester added softly: "Nuts, maybe, but ingenious! Unlike us, the girls seem to know what they're doing."

A lot of time had passed since the stable hands had arrived at the ledge, and Golden Star was completely exhausted. His thin little legs had collapsed, and, after calling and calling – in vain – for his mother, he had lain down. Sunshine's attention was fixed on Diablo.

"We're losing ground here," whispered Chester with a glance at the foal. "He needs nourishment – and quickly!"

Gwendolyn and Ricki had managed to get within ten feet of the horses. Now they stood still.

"Diablo," called Ricki, reaching out her hand cautiously. "Hey, my boy, everything's okay, come here. As you can see, Sunshine has calmed down! Look, Gwen is here, too! Please, Diablo, turn around and come to me!" She kept coaxing her gelding, while Gwendolyn concentrated on the mare.

In a voice that was lyrical and totally in control, Gwen continued singing.

Then, as though in unspoken agreement, the two girls started walking again, very cautiously.

Diablo made a low rumbling noise and suddenly he turned his head toward his owner. Ricki could hardly breathe. Just a little bit farther. Only a few steps more and she'd be able to grab his bridle.

Gwendolyn was also very near her favorite mare and

was tempting her now with one of the treats she always carried in her pockets. She had to move slowly and carefully. Sunshine didn't dare take more than two steps backward. Gwendolyn's nerves were horribly frayed, but she didn't let it show. Finally she was only about two feet away from the mare.

"Okay, Ricki. It's now or never!" she said in song to her new friend. "At the sound of three –" she continued singing. "One... two... three... Now!"

Suddenly – and in unison – the girls grabbed their horses' reins.

Diablo stood still and allowed Ricki to hold on to him, but Sunshine tried to get away from Gwendolyn's grasp. She jerked her head upward in protest and then took a step backward.

"Sunshine!... Stand still! You can't go backward! Ricki, take Diablo away from here. Quickly, please! Take him away!" Gwendolyn's voice lost its calm, and her fear immediately transferred to Sunshine, whose eyes were getting wider by the minute.

Tears ran down Gwendolyn's cheeks. Desperately she pressed the weight of her body against the mare to move her to safety, but the animal continued to resist her.

Meanwhile Ricki had managed to take Diablo away from the edge of the ledge. The farther away from the mare they got, the calmer the horse became.

"Lead him out of the mare's sight as fast as you can," Mario called to her and pointed at the path. "Get off the ledge!" His tone had become gruff and made Ricki nervous.

"C'mon, hurry up, hurry up, come, come," Ricki urged her horse, and finally he began to trot beside her. Ricki

119

halted him after about three hundred feet. Trembling, she glanced back over her shoulder.

Would Gwendolyn make it? Would Golden Star be re-united with his mother?

Scared to death, Ricki buried her face in Diablo's sweaty neck and sobbed bitterly. Her stay at the stud farm wasn't supposed to be like this. No, not at all like this.

*

Mario ran over to Gwendolyn and got to her just as she had exhausted her strength. Her hands were still clutching Sunshine's halter, and she clung to Sunshine's head.

Mario took hold of the mare and pulled with all his might.

"Chester," he screamed. "The foal! Bring the foal here!"

The other groom had the same thought at the same time. Even before Mario had yelled the order at him, Chester had picked up the foal. Now he carried it as fast as he could and put it down on the ground near the mare.

Weakly, the little creature raised his head and looked at his mother with soft, sad eyes, and whinnied.

Sunshine seemed startled, and she looked at her little foal. The mare's nostrils widened as she breathed in the scent of her newborn. All of a sudden, she stopped pulling on the halter.

"Let her go!" Mario and Gwendolyn were surprised by the strength in her grandmother's voice, and looked at each other perplexed.

"But –"

"I said, LET HER GO!"

Doubtfully, Gwen asked: "Is she serious?"

Mario was silent and bit his lips, but after a moment's hesitation, he nodded slightly and then took his hand off the halter.

"But –" Gwen sobbed.

"It's okay. Let her go," said Mario slowly and calmly as he took hold of Gwendolyn's arm and pulled her gently toward him. Step by step, the two of them walked a few feet backward, and then waited anxiously.

For Gwendolyn, these were the most terrible moments of her life.

Golden Star lay motionless, trying one last time to get his mother's attention. His little head nodded and he let out a deep sigh before he tipped over onto his side, exhausted.

Sunshine hesitated and then took one slow step forward. Why didn't her son get up? The other foals that she'd brought into the world had been able to stand up fairly quickly.

Gwendolyn held her breath and grabbed Mario's arm. The man grimaced in pain. Gwendolyn, who knew nothing about Sunshine's bite, had grabbed his arm at exactly the place where he was wounded.

Slowly Sunshine approached her foal. She lowered her head and snorted loudly.

"Well, c'mon, you bad girl," coaxed Chester quietly. He was crouched beside the foal.

Sunshine was close enough to the foal to sniff him, but when he hardly moved as she rubbed his coat with her soft muzzle, she turned away, frustrated, and trotted over to Mrs. Highland, where she stood obediently.

Gwendolyn's grandmother patted the mare's neck, absently, and reached for her halter. Then she waved to Gwen and Mario to come.

"She has rejected the foal, but at least we didn't lose her," Mrs. Highland said as she glanced at the tiny foal that lay cradled in Chester's arms. "Poor little thing, we have to take him home as quickly as possible. We've lost a lot of valuable time."

She walked over to Chester, who had wrapped the little foal in one of the blankets. "Do you think you can manage to carry him awhile? I think Ricki is nearby with Diablo."

Chester nodded before he got up, took a deep breath, and then picked up the foal in his strong arms.

"It's hard to believe that such a thin little thing can weigh so much," he said as he slowly disappeared between the cliffs.

Thoughtfully, Eleanor Highland watched him walk away with the foal. Then, with the authority of the experienced horsewoman she was, she turned to Mario and Gwendolyn, who stood holding Sunshine, and said, "Wait a half hour before you follow us, please. That should give us enough time to get the foal to the trailer – but only if Ricki is still nearby," she added quietly. "Then you two can bring Sunshine there as well. As soon as the foal is home, I'll send William back here to fetch you."

Mario nodded as Gwendolyn, still distraught, stroked her beloved mare on the neck.

Sunshine stood there lethargically, seeming to take no interest in anything that was going on around her. Her emotions were all jumbled. On one hand, she saw her foal as the cause of the terrible suffering she had endured from the difficult birth, and it prevented her from following her motherly instincts. On the other, she mourned the foal who had lain motionless in front of her and with whom she could feel no connection. The mare had become the victim of her own conflicting feelings and no one, least of all Sunshine, could make sense of it.

*

Ricki couldn't decide if she should wait with Diablo on the cliff trail or go back to her friends. She was worried that the mare might freak out if she were to see Diablo, but then she knew that Golden Star couldn't be brought out of the cliffs without Diablo's help. The picture of that helpless little creature finally convinced her to wait a while longer.

After what seemed to her like an eternity, she heard Mrs. Highland call to her, "It's a good thing you're still here. We have the foal with us. Please bring Diablo here. Let's pray that he allows us to place the foal on his back."

Ricki's heart skipped a beat as she saw Chester, breathing heavily, carrying the little foal in his arms.

"If only we had him up there already," said Mrs. Highland, looking at Diablo's broad back doubtfully.

"No problem," panted Chester. "Nothing would surprise me anymore today!"

Ricki swallowed hard. *What did that mean? And why didn't anyone say anything about Sunshine?*

*

Diablo looked bewildered as Chester lifted the foal up to his muzzle.

"So, my boy, I wish I could give you two more of an opportunity to get acquainted, but considering the fact that my arms are already dragging to the ground, and that this young man here must be super hungry, you'll only have

123

time to say hello." Chester then stepped around to Diablo's side, heaved the foal upward, and laid him across the saddle.

Diablo began to prance a bit nervously, but Ricki's calm voice soon got him to stand still again. Curious about the unusual weight he was carrying, Diablo turned his head to the side and glanced back.

"That's pretty strange, isn't it? I bet you've never had a rider like that before." Chester managed to transfer his sense of calm to Diablo, so that the horse began to trot beside Ricki as though carrying a foal on his back was an everyday event.

While Ricki led Diablo through the cliffs, Eleanor Highland and Chester walked on opposite sides of the horse so that they could make sure the little foal didn't slide off.

As they were making their way down the path, no one said a word about Sunshine, but at some point Ricki couldn't stand the mystery any longer. She had to know what had happened.

"What about Sunshine?" she asked softly, without turning around. "Is she still alive?"

Frowning, Eleanor Highland stared at the girl's back and chose her words carefully before she replied. "Sunshine didn't fall off, if that's what you mean. But your horse nearly drove her over the cliff."

Ricki was shocked. She heard the accusation in Mrs. Highland's voice and, for a minute, she wanted to protest, but then thought better of it. After all, if she hadn't ridden to the ledge with Diablo none of this would have happened.

Chester shook his head, unable to understand why his

employer had blamed Diablo when she'd seen for herself how the mare had behaved.

He felt very sorry for Ricki. Deep down, he knew how she was feeling.

*

"There you are! Finally! Wow, it's so cute," exclaimed Cathy as the foal rescue party approached the three waiting teenagers.

"Hey, Diablo makes a good foal carrier," joked Lillian, but Kevin, who only had eyes for Ricki, nudged her hard.

"Shut up. Something must have happened up there," he said seriously. "Look at Ricki's face.... she's really upset."

William sprinted to the trailer and opened up the door. "Where's the mare?" he asked, letting down the ramp.

"Mario and Gwen are bringing her. We're going to drive the foal home immediately, and afterward, you'll return here to pick the three of them up."

William looked at Mrs. Highland with raised eyebrows. Her voice had the old tone of icy superiority again. "Well," he asked merrily, "didn't we have an agreement?" The woman just looked at him angrily.

"Forget about the agreement!" she snapped back at him. "Just do your work and leave me alone for the rest of the day!"

She stomped around the vehicle with a haughty air, and sat down in the passenger seat, where she waited impatiently for William to get in.

*

125

Only after Ricki had led Diablo into the trailer did they lift the foal down from the gelding's back. Gently, Chester and William laid the little animal onto the straw.

"So, let's get going," urged Chester and crouched down beside Golden Star.

"Come on, let's take Diablo back home, too," said William kindly, but Ricki shook her head firmly.

"Thank you, that's really nice of you, but I think it will be better if I ride."

Sadly, the girl led her horse back down the trailer ramp. When she was at the bottom, she turned and called to the two men, "Please tell Mrs. Highland that I'm sorry about what happened up there. Tell her that I never wanted that to happen." Ricki's voice broke, and as tears welled up in her eyes, she swung herself into the saddle and trotted off quickly on Diablo without another word.

From the door of the trailer, William watched her ride unhappily away. "*Now* what's wrong? I don't understand anything anymore!"

Chester got up and nudged him down the ramp. "Just drive. Every minute counts! I'll explain everything to you when we get home, okay?"

*

"Hey, what's going on with Ricki?" asked Lillian, puzzled, as she saw Diablo race away.

Kevin turned around with a start. "I have no idea, but I'll know soon!" Without bothering with stirrups, he jumped into Sharazan's saddle and raced after Diablo. *Haven't we already done this once today?* he thought, as his horse broke into a gallop.

126

Lillian and Cathy stayed behind with Holli, Rashid, and Black Jack.

"Actually, they could have taken you and your injured ankle back home, too," said Lillian and gave Cathy a meaningful look.

"Oh, whatever. First of all, they didn't know anything about it, and secondly, I have a feeling that Mrs. Highland is in a really bad mood. Let's just wait for Gwen and Mario," responded Cathy.

"We haven't waited for anyone in a long time, have we?" Lillian grinned broadly.

"You know what, I'm really starving," exclaimed Cathy. "Do you think we have a chance of getting anything to eat today?"

"Sure! Now everything makes sense!" Lillian chuckled. "Mrs. Highland was in a bad mood because she was hungry. It was low blood sugar!"

Lillian and Cathy began to laugh simultaneously. They were still giggling as Mario and Gwendolyn emerged from the cliffs with Sunshine.

"Uh-oh!" said Lillian when she saw Gwen's pale, serious face. "She doesn't look any better than Ricki did!"

"Well, at least maybe now we'll find out what happened," countered Cathy and stretched her sore back.

*

"Ricki! Wait!" Kevin, on Sharazan, tried to cut off Diablo, who had galloped around a long curve, but he only gained a few feet.

"What's wrong? Ricki, if you don't stop I'm really going to get mad!" yelled Kevin. Diablo's rider sighed loudly and pulled in the reins gently. Without turning around, she waited for Kevin to catch up.

The boy looked at his girlfriend with concern, and waited silently for her to tell him why she had just ridden off alone. But Ricki just stared straight ahead and said nothing.

Kevin felt so sorry for her. Leaning toward her, he laid his hand on her arm. "No matter what it is, I'm listening," he said before he dismounted. "C'mon, let's walk awhile." He reached out his hand gallantly to help her down from the saddle, but Ricki paid him no attention and just slid out of the saddle sideways.

She held tightly to the reins for fear that Diablo would run off again.

"C'mon, tell me. I can't help you unless you tell me what's wrong," urged Kevin with a gentle smile.

Ricki's shoulders began to jerk involuntarily and without saying any more, Kevin just took his girlfriend in his arms. Not able to keep her tears back anymore, Ricki sobbed her heart out on his shoulder.

She told him how she had heard Chester and his colleagues talking, and how she had then taken off on Diablo to search for Sunshine, and how she had found the mare lying on the ledge. After that she told him about the horrible meeting between Diablo and the mare, then the birth of the foal, and ended with the fiasco at the edge of the cliffs, which had totally unnerved Sunshine.

"...And I know that Mrs. Highland blames me for everything because I brought Diablo onto the ledge. But I just wanted to help. I just wanted him to bring Golden Star back to the trailer unhurt. I... Oh, Kevin, I want to go home so bad. Please, let's ride home or someplace else. I can't go back to the estate. Can you understand that?" She raised her eyes, red from crying, and looked pleadingly at Kevin.

The boy, who was slightly taller than she, gently rested his chin on her hair. He could understand how sad she felt right now, but he had no idea how he could grant her wish.

"I know what you mean, Ricki, but at the moment, we have no choice but to return to the estate," he said softly and felt her stiffen in defiance. He placed a kiss on her forehead and said, "I promise you, tomorrow I'll talk with Mrs. Highland and tell her everything. She wouldn't really listen to me today anyway. Her worries about Sunshine and, even more, with the foal, will take up all of her time."

Ricki stared into the distance. "The foal," she whispered. "It's a wonderful creature and it doesn't have a real mother any more. Darn, I feel sick."

She leaned against Kevin's chest and tried to take deep breaths to get rid of the nausea. Finally the fresh evening air did just that.

"It's getting dark – we'd better get started," said Kevin, and there was so much tenderness and concern in his voice that Ricki couldn't do anything else but comply.

"Okay," she whispered tonelessly and climbed, this time somewhat heavily, into Diablo's saddle. "Considering that I was supposed to stay in bed for two days, I've really done a lot today. I'm exhausted."

*

Gwendolyn had decided to make her way back to the stud farm on horseback with Lillian and Cathy, while Mario stayed with Sunshine waiting for William to pick them up. She had seen Ricki riding off hastily and was worried about her, and so she was glad that Kevin had ridden after her.

"Ricki must be feeling terrible," Gwen said to the girls as they rode. "I'm sure that my grandmother said something awful to her. You know, she really is a warmhearted person, but she's always saying things that hurt others without meaning to. I have to talk with her about that when we get back home."

"I hope the foal is okay," Lillian wished aloud, saying what the three of them had been thinking the whole time.

"And I hope that Sunshine isn't going to stay this way," added Gwendolyn. Then the girls rode the rest of the way back in silence.

*

It was already dark when Kevin and Ricki arrived at the stud farm.

"Well, finally!" Lillian breathed a sigh of relief. "I was beginning to think you were never coming back."

"I would have preferred not to," said Ricki quietly, and slid down from the saddle. "How's the foal?" she wanted to know right away, as she led her horse to the stable.

"Chester is with him and he fed him some prepared food. He has to do that every two hours now," Cathy reported. "Mario tried to milk Sunshine, so that the little guy could get some real mother's milk, but the mare is so mean that she lays back her ears as soon as she sees him coming. She won't let anyone but Gwen into her stall, and she won't let even Gwen milk her."

130

Kevin gave Cathy a warning glance and nodded slightly in Ricki's direction. He mouthed the words shut up, and Cathy understood. *Why do I always have to say the first thing that comes into my head ?* she chastised herself.

Quickly she tried to save what she could. "By the way, Gwen talked to her grandmother. She isn't mad at you anymore, and she wants to talk with you tonight."

Ricki groaned. "Oh no, not that! The only thing I want to do is go to bed and sleep!"

Her friends all nodded in sympathy.

"Then get going!" said Lillian and gave her a gentle shove on her back. "We'll take care of Diablo and Sharazan, and when they've gotten their well-deserved feed and are safe in their stalls, we'll go to bed, too. I think a good night's sleep will make us all feel better."

Ricki nodded and patted Diablo gently before handing Lillian the reins. "Cathy, Kevin told me that you had an accident with your ankle. How are you?"

Her girlfriend grinned. "As you can see, I'm still alive, and I can limp around on it. Nothing serious. Go to bed, Ricki, and don't worry so much. Tomorrow everything will look much better."

That would be great, thought Ricki as she wearily shuffled along the corridor of the stable. Once outside she was surrounded by a warm summer night with hundreds of golden stars in the sky.

"Golden Star," she said softly to herself. "I have to see him one more time. I have to see if he's okay. Maybe then I can go to sleep and not worry about him so much."

Summoning her strength, she turned and walked toward the mares' stable instead of going in the house, where her comfortable bed was waiting for her.

131

When she got there, she pressed down the safety latch and went in. She stood in the partially lit corridor.

Ricki didn't know if the foal was here or had been taken to another stable, but she assumed that he would be near Sunshine, even if the mare rejected him, and that's exactly the way it was.

She discovered the little foal in a wonderful roomy stall that was about forty feet from Sunshine's stall. Chester sat beside him and fed him with a baby bottle.

When Chester saw Ricki, he flashed her a broad smile. "He's drinking, and that's the most important thing," he said quietly so as not to upset the foal or the other mares in the stable.

Longingly Ricki watched the wonderful golden brown creature nudging the nipple of the bottle greedily.

"Oh, come on in," whispered Chester, who had understood Ricki's look. He moved a little to the side and the girl sat down beside him.

"Here, hold this," he said, and put the milk bottle into her hand. He could sense that it was very important for Ricki to feel how alive the foal was in order to let go of her feelings of guilt.

"Cathy said that you have to feed the little guy every two hours. Is that true?" she asked shyly.

Chester nodded. "Watch out, he's done! So, you little imp, stop. We have to clean you up a bit." Chester wiped the little mouth and nose with a clean rag before he left the foal in peace.

"Now he can sleep a bit, our future stud stallion," the stable groom said, and got up a little awkwardly. He'd been sitting there so long his legs had gone to sleep and he was a little stiff.

Ricki looked at the foal, who had lain down again on his side. "I would love to stay here," she whispered softly and put her hands on the warm soft coat of the animal.

Chester's heart went out to her. This girl had so much love for horses. He remembered what Gwen had said to him when they brought the foal home: "If anyone's earned the right to stay the night with the little foal, it's Ricki, without a doubt."

Without considering the trouble that he was going to be in with Mrs. Highland when she found out about this, Chester nodded encouragingly to Ricki.

"I think the little guy will be very lonely tonight. If you want to –"

Ricki swallowed a yelp of joy. She gave the groom a big hug around the neck and kissed his cheek.

"Thanks, Chester, thank you, thank you, thank you! I don't know what to say," she stammered. She knew he would have to come up with a good excuse for his employer to explain why he was giving her this permission.

"Are you hungry?" the groom asked.

Ricki shrugged her shoulders. "I don't really know... I guess I am, a little," she said hesitantly.

"Hmm," replied Chester, and disappeared. A few minutes later he reappeared in front of the stall.

"Here, I had some stuff in my secret stash," he grinned and held out a small salami and a large roll. "You have to have some provisions for long nights in the stable. I have a bottle of water, too. When you're done with it, put it under the bench in the corridor. Mrs. Highland doesn't like to see glass bottles in the stable. Tomorrow morning I'll come and get it. Here are two blankets for you."

Ricki nodded gratefully. Chester was really a nice guy.

As she bit hungrily into the salami, the groom said good-bye. "Well, see ya. I'll be back in two hours." Chester waved at her and smiled, and then he closed the stall's sliding door carefully.

"Good night, you two," he whispered softly, and walked down the stable corridor and out into the night. He was going to rest until it was time to give the foal his next feeding.

Ricki heard his steps echoing down the corridor and was glad that the groom had left the emergency light on. There was just enough light for her to watch the foal.

"Oh, you are so beautiful," she murmured, and as she laid down beside Golden Star she felt a sense of happiness that she'd never experienced in her young life. Well, once before... when she got Diablo from Jake. She had felt this happy then... only it was different somehow.

She put her hand tenderly on the newborn's coat and closed her eyes.

"Sleep well into a wonderful life, free from worry, my little Golden Star," she whispered as she drifted into a deep, dreamless, untroubled sleep.

Chapter 9

"Hey, little lady, wake up! You want to feed him, don't you?" Chester shook Ricki's shoulder lightly.

The girl looked at him, eyes heavy with sleep, but seconds later she was wide awake.

"Wow, are the two hours up already?" she asked, amazed. Chester nodded, grinning at her.

"Oh, yeah, the nights are short when you're caring for a foal. Here, you know how to do it."

He held the milk bottle out to her. "And be careful that he doesn't get any milk up his nose with his greedy drinking. We definitely don't want the youngster to suffocate on us, do we?"

Golden Star had gotten up into a drinking position and was sucking on the nipple avidly. Ricki was engrossed in the whole process.

"If only Sunshine would let him nurse," she whispered.

"Now don't worry about that," Chester comforted her. "This little guy isn't the first foal we've raised with a bottle. He'll grow up big and strong, regardless. I promise you!"

Ricki looked at the groom doubtfully. "Honest? Or are you just trying to make me feel better?" she asked.

"I wouldn't lie to a colleague," he said with a merry twinkle in his eyes.

"Then that's okay," responded Ricki and smiled back at him. Nevertheless, an idea had taken shape in her mind that she couldn't get rid of.

*

It was past one A.M. when Chester left again.

Ricki was dead tired and could have fallen asleep on her feet. However, the idea she was mulling over just wouldn't leave her alone.

Filled with excitement, she stared at the little foal lying at her feet and then in the direction of Sunshine's stall.

She just couldn't accept that the mare wouldn't acknowledge her own foal. After all, she had given birth to it under a lot of pain, just as she had given birth to so many foals before him. Ricki also didn't want to accept that Diablo was the reason Sunshine had rejected her foal.

Ricki got up carefully so as not to disturb the foal, opened the stall door, and quietly stepped out into the corridor.

She listened intently in the dark hallway, but all she heard was a soft snoring sound. Chester seemed to be asleep.

Ricki smiled. She was sure that Chester would have slept beside the foal all night if she wasn't there, instead of in the small feed room, where he had set up his cot.

Quietly she ran along the stalls where Isis and Aida dozed with their heads hanging. A little farther along, Jasmine was lying in the straw with her two-month-old foal Glamour, sleeping without a care in the world.

136

In nature the mares would never be able to sleep so deeply, thought Ricki. They'd be keeping an ear open for danger. But here they knew they and their foals were safe.

She found it hard to tear herself away from the tranquil sight. But only a few more feet and she would be standing in front of Sunshine's stall.

Ricki inhaled deeply. From Jasmine's stall she could recognize the mare in the dim light. She saw her pacing around in her stall, her ears continuously fluttering back and forth.

Now the mare had seen Ricki, too, and was getting nervous. What was this human stranger doing in the stable at night? Where was Chester? Where was Mario?

Sunshine kicked against the wall with her hoof, and Ricki was worried that the animal would wake Chester, but she could hear his rhythmic snoring coming from the feed room.

Although she was extremely nervous, Ricki knew that she wouldn't find any peace if she didn't at least try what she had worked out in her mind. So she went on hesitantly.

Sunshine drew in the scent of the girl with wide-open nostrils and associated her immediately with the painful events at the cliffs. However, there was also something else, something that filled her with a deep sadness. Somehow the girl's scent carried with it the memory of her foal.

The mare turned away. She didn't want to think about her foal, which had lain so still in front of her.

Ricki had come close enough, and now she began to speak softly to the mare.

"Hello, Sunshine. Do you recognize me? We went through a lot together yesterday, didn't we? I can't tell you

137

how glad I am you're alive. Why did you run away? You could have had your foal here in the stall, nice and cozy."

Sunshine's ears turned toward the soft human voice that, she recalled, had comforted her so much at the birth of her foal. But she knew that she hated this human. The black devil that had caused her so much pain belonged to her. However, the girl's voice made her feel secure. How should she react now?

The mare kept looking around the stall. Ricki didn't seem to be dangerous, and the black monster was nowhere to be seen.

Slowly Sunshine began to relax. She listened closely to the loving words Ricki spoke to her, and finally she even dared to take a few steps toward the girl, sticking her neck out over the door of the stall to allow the girl to gently stroke her muzzle with her fingertips.

"See, it's going to be all right. I won't hurt you," Ricki smiled and said soothingly, while she quickly thought over her plan. She had to win the mare's trust. Without that trust, she wouldn't even be able to enter her stall safely.

After about thirty minutes, Ricki left Sunshine and slipped back into the stall where Golden Star lay. Soon it would be time for another feeding. She wanted to catch a little more sleep until then.

Just as Chester had predicted, the night would be a long one.

*

Although her body was letting her know how exhausted she was, she was much too excited to sleep.

"Your bed is a little uncomfortable, isn't it?" Chester had

asked her earlier – and he was right – but she wouldn't have traded her place in the stall for anything.

Now she got up again and walked wearily toward Sunshine's stall. The mare glanced at her, surprised but no longer frightened.

"See? I told you everything would be okay," Ricki whispered and pulled a treat out of her jeans pocket. She had taken a few from a basket of horse snacks she found on a bench in the corridor, probably left there by Gwendolyn.

Sunshine stretched out her neck. She loved these secret little treats that before now she'd received only from Gwen.

Ricki felt the mare's soft lips stroking her palm gently, as the mare accepted the present.

The girl gave Sunshine a few minutes to get used to her and then she slowly lifted the latch on the stall and slid the door open slightly.

Immediately Sunshine jumped back into the corner and stuck out her hind quarter toward Ricki as a warning.

Don't get too close! she seemed to be saying. *Giving me a treat doesn't give you the right to enter my private space! Go away!*

Ricki waited awhile and stood completely still, but her lips continually moved as she spoke comforting words to the mare. All the while she watched Sunshine, who stood defensively in the corner. Her udder was very full, and the milk was beginning to drip from the teats. Chester had tried to milk the mare, but in vain. Sunshine wouldn't let him near her.

"You know what," said Ricki softly, "your milk is wasting away, dripping into the straw, and your foal has to drink man-made stuff, although it would be much healthier for him to get your milk. Do you think that's right? And anyway, it must be very painful for you when your udder is so full. Why don't you at least let someone take your milk? You would feel so much better, my good –"

Sunshine began to realize that Ricki was very much like her own beloved Gwendolyn, and therefore she turned slowly around toward her again. She stretched out her neck and began to sniff Ricki from top to bottom.

Cautiously Ricki opened the door a little more and took one step toward the mare, who was eyeing her skeptically.

Ricki sighed. "Are you always like this, or did Diablo make you so scared that you're afraid to trust anyone anymore?" she asked softly. "Try to trust me just a little bit. I won't hurt you. I only want you – Oh, Sunshine, don't make this so difficult for yourself and me. Only a few stalls away, your foal is lying in the straw missing you! Don't you feel the same way? Have you forgotten your foal?"

Suddenly she remembered the children's song that Gwendolyn had sung on the cliffs. Should she take the chance? Her voice wasn't very good, but she should be able to sing a children's song. It couldn't be that hard!

So Ricki began to hum the melody that had soothed Sunshine before.

Huh? What's going on? Sunshine pointed her ears and looked hard at Ricki. That song... oh, how she loves that melody, although it sounds a little different when Gwen sings it.

After listening attentively for a while, the mare relaxed and came closer. She seemed convinced that the song guaranteed her the safety she longed for. Gently she probed Ricki's face with her soft muzzle.

Calmly and slowly Ricki raised her hand and placed it on Sunshine's neck, and the animal allowed her to do it

140

without backing away. The mare had longed for the close-
ness of a kind human, but since yesterday she had associated people with the pain caused by that black giant, and was
so afraid that someone would hurt her again.

But now everything was okay. Everything was as it had
always been, before she'd left the stable and gone to that
terrible place near the cliffs, where she had experienced
fear and pain.

Ricki sensed the change that was taking place within the
mare at this moment and she gave her plenty of time so that
she could feel safe and secure.

"Are you okay again?" Sunshine answered playfully by
poking Ricki in the chest with her muzzle.

Ricki was elated. She had overcome the first hurdle, and
she sensed that the moment had come to do what she had
intended to do throughout the night.

Determined, she took hold of Sunshine's halter, slid
open the door of the stall as far as it would go, and led the
mare out onto the corridor.

Sunshine glanced at the girl, but as she stood beside her
she wasn't afraid anymore. She knew she didn't have anything to fear from Ricki.

"Let's go," whispered the girl and pulled on the halter to
urge Sunshine forward. As Ricki heard the sound of
Sunshine's hooves on the pavement, she kept worrying that
Chester would wake up, realize what was happening, and
suddenly appear in the stall. She was certain he wouldn't
allow what was going to happen next. The risk that something would go wrong was too great.

Ricki's heart beat wildly. She knew it wasn't right to try
anything risky with these animals that didn't belong to her,
and she knew that a failure would make things really diffi-

cult for her. However, she believed that what she was doing was right.

Ricki halted Sunshine. They were almost in front of the stall where the foal lay sleeping peacefully.

Sunshine's ears twitched nervously. She shook her head and snorted. Then she opened her nostrils wide and breathed in the scent of her foal, who was sleeping behind the stall gate.

For an instant she was startled. She associated the scent with the painful events on the cliffs. But just as quickly as these feelings had flared up, her maternal instincts awakened, and with each additional breath Sunshine took, they multiplied and pushed aside the memories of the painful birth and the terrible experience with Diablo.

And now? What's going to happen next? Ricki asked herself, anxiously biting her lips. But before she could think of anything practical, Sunshine and Golden Star decided for her.

The little legs of the foal began to move while he slept. Perhaps in a dream he was trotting across a meadow. Sunshine pushed closer to the stall, saw her sleeping foal, and gave a very soft, gentle whinny. It was the whinny of a mare calling her colt.

Golden Star jerked involuntary, but as his mother called again, he opened his eyes. *Huh! Wasn't that –?* The little guy got up quickly onto his legs. Instinct told him that he belonged to this mare who kept whinnying lowly at him.

Excitedly, Sunshine started to sniff around the door of the stall, searching desperately for a way to get to her foal.

"Be quiet, my girl, otherwise we'll wake up Chester, and who knows what will happen then," Ricki begged the mare, who didn't seem to share her concerns.

142

The animal shoved her muzzle through the opening between the slats in the door as far as she could, to try to make contact with Golden Star. Awkwardly and a little stiffly, the foal went straight to his mother, stretched his neck, and pressed his little muzzle against the metal that was keeping them apart.

Ricki watched this union of mare and foal with a lump in her throat. And when she saw Sunshine place her body parallel to the wall as if she was offering him her milk, Ricki decided to risk the last step. Although Sunshine showed no indication of any further rejection, Ricki swallowed hard as she opened the stall door.

Sunshine almost pressed her against the wall as she forced her way to her foal, but Ricki held on to the halter firmly so that she could lead the mare out of the stall again quickly if things went badly.

It has to work, it just has to work. C'mon, you can't mess this up, thought Ricki. She would never forget these tense moments, but soon she realized that her doubts were unfounded.

Sunshine had gone to her foal and bent her head over his back protectively. Carefully the mare touched his warm coat with her muzzle and shook her head trying to free herself from Ricki's hold. *Let me go,* her glance at Ricki seemed to say.

"Well," the teenager whispered softly, "are you two getting along?" Ricki couldn't make herself release the mare just yet, but after a few minutes, she took a deep breath, let go of the mare, and stepped back slowly.

Golden Star lowered his head and began to probe Sunshine's belly. Instinct told him that there must be something there that would take away the hunger pangs.

Gently Sunshine helped him by poking him toward her udder. She stood with her hind legs spread so that the little fellow could get to the milk easily. Quietly she sniffed along his flanks while Golden Star intuitively searched for a teat with his mouth. When he found it, he began to drink his mother's milk, his tail wagging back and forth in contentment.

Sunshine glanced at Ricki proudly. *Well, what do you think of us?* her eyes asked. Ricki had to hold on to the wall of the stall to keep her trembling knees from buckling.

I won't cry again, she thought, deeply moved by the sight before her. But the tears streaked down her cheeks anyway.

Yes, I will! she said to herself. *These are tears of joy, and they're always allowed!* she added stubbornly.

*

When Chester stumbled sleepily along the stable corridor about three o'clock in the morning, on his way to feed the foal, he saw immediately that Sunshine's stall was empty.

Instantly he became wide awake. "Oh, no! Where is she?!" he mumbled, pinching his arm to make sure he wasn't dreaming.

As he frantically looked up and down the corridor, his mind was racing. *This just can't be happening! She can't have disappeared into thin air! The stall is locked, and I would have noticed if a stranger had come into the stable. She won't let anyone near her anyway, but she's not in the corridor either! Now Mrs. Highland will go completely ballistic!*

He glanced down at the milk bottle in his hand and remembered where he had been going. He ran quickly down the corridor. *Ricki can feed the little guy while I let Mrs. H. know what happened,* he thought. He felt sick to his stomach just thinking about how she would react.

As he got to the foal's stall, he stopped short and wondered if he was hallucinating. He began to sputter, "Am I completely crazy? This isn't possible! No! How –?"

There, in the stall, Sunshine stood calmly with her head lowered to her contented foal, who was sleeping on the straw, while Ricki, slumped in the corner against the wall, slept soundly.

Chester dropped the milk bottle and rubbed his hand over his eyes. Suddenly he understood everything, and he shook his head again, while he watched the sleeping Ricki. *That girl really has guts,* he thought.

Ricki woke up and looked up at Chester with half-opened eyes. "Is it time to feed him?" she asked, but Chester just gestured no.

"Sunshine has already taken care of it, I assume," he answered softly and smiled as Ricki, with her eyes closed again, just nodded.

"I guess she loves him after all," mumbled the girl with a happy look on her face.

"Sleep, Ricki," Chester whispered, his voice breaking with emotion. "You deserve it. You've really worked a miracle."

The girl nodded again, even though Chester's words hadn't reached her. She was too far away, in the land of dreams, where Diablo, Sunshine, and Golden Star galloped together over the paddocks of Highland Farms Estate, expressing their love of life with every stride.

*

Early morning light was beginning to show. Gwendolyn, unable to sleep because of her concerns for Sunshine and her foal, had tossed and turned in bed the whole night. She decided she might as well get up.

She left her room quietly, so as not to wake anyone, but as she tiptoed into the kitchen to get something for breakfast, she came upon her grandmother, who was already at the table with a steaming cup of coffee in front of her.

"Good morning, Granny. What are you doing here at this time of morning?" Gwendolyn asked, taking a piece of cinnamon toast from the serving plate.

Her grandmother looked back at her with very tired eyes. "Good morning," she said. "I couldn't sleep."

"Neither could I. I hope the little guy drank well during the night," said Gwendolyn with her cheeks full.

Eleanor Highland nodded. "I'm going to go check on him right after breakfast."

"Great, I'll go with you! What are you going to name him?" she asked her grandmother expectantly.

"Hmm, I'm not sure yet, but I'm leaning toward Galahad," Mrs. Highland replied thoughtfully.

"Oh."

"What does that 'Oh' mean? Don't you like the name?" said her grandmother.

"Yeaaaah," answered Gwendolyn slowly, "It's okay." Then she looked up in surprise as the kitchen door opened and Ricki's friends came in excitedly.

"Some more people who couldn't sleep," she grinned, but Kevin looked at her seriously before he turned to Mrs. Highland.

146

"Good morning," he wished her, although he couldn't hide his feelings.

"What's up?" asked Gwendolyn, and put down the glass of juice she had been holding.

"Ricki's gone!" exploded Cathy.

"Or more exactly, we don't know if she was even in her bed. It looks totally unused!" Lillian added.

"Not again!" Abruptly Mrs. Highland pushed her cup aside and got up. "Come with me!" she ordered, and walked briskly out of the kitchen, as the friends glanced at each other full of unspoken questions.

"Where are you going?" Gwendolyn asked, a little out of breath, as she and the others followed her grandmother out of the house and over to the guests' stable.

"I want to see if her horse is still in his stall. If he's gone too, then I won't be so worried!"

"But if she was going for a ride, she would have woken us up so that we could go with her," interrupted Kevin.

But Eleanor Highland didn't seem to care. She was beginning to wonder how she could have ever thought of inviting these children to the farm. Her friend Carlotta had spoken well of them, but in the short time they'd been there, there'd been nothing but trouble.

Determinedly, she opened the door to the guests' stable and, with the teenagers in tow, marched silently past Mario, who glanced up at her with a puzzled expression.

"Good morning, Mrs. Highland," he called after her, looking at his watch.

"Diablo is here," called Gwendolyn and got a nasty look from her grandmother in return.

"I'm not blind!" She turned around immediately and raced out of the stable, followed by the four teenagers.

147

What was that all about? Mario wondered. And so did Diablo, Holli, Rashid, and Sharazan. Their usual morning greeting was missing.

*

"Who does that girl think she is," growled Eleanor Highland to herself. "She comes and goes as she likes and turns everything here upside down! That has to stop! First, I'll check on the foal and Sunshine, and then I'll think over what to do about her!"

"Uh-oh," said Gwendolyn ominously. "I think this is going to be a bad day!"

Lillian just looked at her contritely. "I don't know what Ricki's thinking right now, but I have a sneaking suspicion your grandmother isn't too pleased that we're here," she replied.

"Maybe William can take us home today." Cathy began, but Gwendolyn shook her head.

"Oh, no, you guys! I was so excited about you coming for a visit!

"I would like to ask you all to be quiet in the mares' stable!" Mrs. Highland said before she opened the door.

The teenagers all nodded. "Absolutely!"

They entered on tiptoe, and then walked by the wide rows of stalls.

Chester was just about to mix the oats with the mineral additives in the feed room when he realized that he was no longer alone.

"Well, good morning," he greeted his employer warmly. All he got in return was a curt nod.

"How are the foal and Sunshine doing?" she asked him

148

instead of a greeting. But when she saw that the mare's stall was empty, she demanded to know, "Where is she?"

Chester put his fingers to his lips. "Shhhh," he said, smiling warmly, making the kids grin. "Sunshine is in another stall."

"That is what I assumed! Why?" Mrs. Highland brusquely asked. Instead of an answer, Chester just motioned her to follow him.

Angrily she followed the groom, but after a few feet her pace slowed. She could see Sunshine in the stall where the little foal had been yesterday.

"What is going on?"

"Shhhh... quiet!" urged Chester, and made his morning guests approach the stall silently.

When they got close, five pairs of eyes stared in total disbelief at Ricki, who was still asleep, the foal's head in her lap. Above them, the mare watched protectively.

Touched by the scene, Gwendolyn reached for her grandmother's hand, and for once Eleanor Highland was speechless.

She glanced at Chester questioningly, and he just pointed at Ricki.

"Her?" she asked. "She brought the two of them together during the night? Well, I believe I've completely misjudged that girl."

Chester nodded in agreement and looked at Ricki's friends, who were beaming and hugging each other.

"What's the foal's name, by the way?" asked Cathy quietly, and just as quietly Mrs. Highland answered with a grateful look at Ricki, "What a question! Why, Golden Star, of course!"

Gwendolyn smiled at that, while Ricki forced herself to

go on pretending to be asleep, although, inside, she was bursting with joy. *And I'm going to figure out how to solve the problem between Sunshine and Diablo, too,* she thought, as her friends and her hostess tiptoed away so as not to wake her.

After the stable door closed, Chester said softly, "You can open your eyes now. They've all gone!"

Ricki grinned at him. "Just for now, I'm going to enjoy having Golden Star all to myself, because later, they'll be all over him. But who can blame them. After all, he is one of the most beautiful foals in the world!"